The
Forgotten God

Editing by Belle Manuel

First Edition 2023

ISBN 979-8-9873772-0-8

Published by SthenoType
Medford, NJ 08055
www.SthenoType.com

Thank you to all those that supported and encouraged me along the way.

"Oftentimes, it is not the numbers that win the victory, but those that charge forward with the most vigor"
Norse wisdom

Prologue

A wooden prow cut through the frigid water of the Labrador Sea. On the boat, around 30 Norse explorers were searching for land.

"Are you sure this is the way, sir?" a crewman asked.

"Bjarni mapped the voyage well, the return trip anyway," the steersman answered.

Leif Erikson was confident he would find the land and establish a merchant route when a settlement was founded. The stories of trees and wineberries demanded exploration, and promised a boon to their settlements throughout Greenland, which lacked many resources. His father, Erik the Red, should have been leading this voyage, but he was injured before departure and entrusted it to Leif, who was desperate to succeed.

Supplies had dwindled during the voyage, as most of the cargo on their knarr was tools for gathering resources and constructing a settlement. Food had been tough to come by, but the occasional ringed seal provided meat. Fresh water was waning, however.

"Land!" a deckhand called out, pointing to the south.

An hour later, the boat was moored, and Leif's crew was working to unload their cargo. Leif sent scouts to find any other inhabitants, animal trails, or water sources. After some searching the scouts were distraught to have not found much. There appeared to be no other settlements nearby, which seemed to be because there was little wildlife activity here.

"He's not going to be happy," one of the scouts said, defeated. He was a young man, barely a beard on his chin.

"We don't have the supplies to make another trip, we need to continue south and find food. The fish and birds will sustain us for a bit," the eldest of the group, Tyrker, intoned with his face hard and determined.

"And what of the water?"

Sigh. "The sea water here is drinkable, for a little while. We may be able to dig a well or find a fissure somewhere if we keep looking. Let us rest here and eat some of these berries to regain our strength before we head back."

The men had found patches of various berries, and assumed these were the wineberries they were told about by the explorer, Bjarni, who had claimed to find this land after being blown about by a storm. There were trees in the distance as well to the south, which Tyrker hoped contained the wildlife they would need. A while after eating the berries the men indeed felt a bit tipsy, likely because the season had ended for these berries and they appeared to be late on the vine.

"Knew we shouldn't have set out until Erik had healed. Leif was too eager to claim glory and we're going to pay his price." The young scout growled bitterly while staring at the ground.

"Careful Grimur, the Lawspeakers wouldn't take kindly to you talking about the steersman that way," Arne warned.

"Neither would Erik or me," Tyrker said quietly.

"You know I'm right. This was a doomed mission from the beginning and having to listen to him and watch him stride about while knowing he's a fool only worsens it."

"You've had too many berries," Arne said hurriedly. "Hold your tongue!"

"Bah. I will hold Leif's tongue when I cut it from him. I won't be alone, there's others that'll join."

"Have you discussed this with others?" Tyrker challenged.

"They've brought it to me!"

Tyrker looked to Arne, and Arne nodded. Tyrker may not be a Lawspeaker, but he knew the law. As the skipper on this trip, and Leif's adoptive father, he could not allow a mutiny. With a flick of his head, he signaled Arne, who grabbed Grimur and held him to the ground.

"What is this?!" Grimur demanded.

"For treason against your steersman, I sentence you to death by our custom." Tyrker informed him sadly.

"Are you mad?! Get off me. I was only..."

Grimur's protests were cut off by Tyrker's axe. His blow was mighty, cracking the stone beneath the body.

"What do we tell Leif?"

"We tell him that Grimur became drunk on the berries and attacked us. We don't need him worrying about traitors, we can flush them out." Tyrker said as he cleaned his axe. He cocked his head and listened. "Do you hear water?"

"I think that's the blood draining through the rock."

"Not that fast it isn't."

They moved the body and through the crack in the rock saw water beginning to bubble through. After cleaning the rock and breaking away more they found a spring where they had struck.

◈ ◈ ◈

Odin sat on his throne in Gladsheim, looking to the other gods gathered.

"High Council, we find ourselves in a position that requires action. As you know, our followers have begun abandoning us for a new god. While we are still strong, I fear that we will continue to weaken as our offerings cease. Beyond that, Ragnarok looms. The death of Balder is the first sign of things to come, and from here I have foreseen the end."

"Well, thanks for that cheery outlook," said Bragi. "I notice some are missing from this Council."

"Yes. I believe we can forestall Ragnarok. Through the whisperings of Mimir I have found a way to change our fates, though it isn't without cost."

"Then tell us," said Viðar.

"Balder's death will lead to hasty judgement and actions we can't come back from."

"Didn't you have a child, grow them into adulthood, and have him slay Hoth in his first day of life as retribution?" asked Bragi.

"Yes."

"And bind Loki with his own son's entrails for his actions in the death?" asked Vidar.

"Yes. Hence the need for a chance to cool our minds and have this meeting!" Odin's eye flashed grey with anger.

"Okay. We're listening."

"Mimir, tell them our plan."

A silent, decomposing head looked over the crowd, hanging from Odin's belt. The faintest whisper, as if wind from a distant shore could be heard.

"Right, forgot, he's not much for public speaking. The logic is sound and we've considered many paths it may take, but I do believe we can stop Ragnarok and save the realms. Now, generally messing with prophecy is a tricky business and is prone to backfiring, but we believe the Norns will accept our sacrifice as a price."

The gods leaned forward as Odin told them the plan.

Ava Tillmann rode in the passenger seat of her dad's rental car with her headphones in and watching videos on her phone. They were driving up the coast of Newfoundland to visit a small but, according to her dad, "exciting" dig site.

Her father, Dr. Harrison Tillmann, was a history professor at a university in their town. He tended to get excited by discoveries regularly, but he rarely got a chance to go into the field. His specialty was medieval archaeology, and without much of that to dig up in North America plus a wife who was unwilling to move, he was forced to put his education to use teaching students about other people's findings.

Ava's brother, Jake, and his friend, Bill, were along as well. The boys were annoying to Ava at the best of times, but a two-hour flight and now a five-hour car ride were straining her ability to act calm in front of her dad. While they hadn't said much to her directly, she just knew their stifled laughter and not-so-quiet chatter from the backseat involved jokes at her expense. She was tuning them out by snacking on Smarties and watching Kuhlr videos, mostly of the existential teenage crisis variety. She found they calmed her.

Remembering the time my boyfriend cheated on me, and I dumped 25 pounds of instant mashed potatoes in his trunk and left it open in the rain was written on the screen of this video, over the face of a pretty girl around 19 years old with emo music playing over it. The next video was a boy that looked about her age, 13, with head in hands responding loudly to the revelation that the color orange derived its name from the fruit, not the other way around.

"You know, this is the first well they've found at this site?" her dad asked.

"Hmm?" Ava answered distractedly.

"There haven't been any other wells found at the Viking site. Around 100 people likely lived there and we hadn't found a fresh water source yet. We just assumed it had been eroded or been destroyed..." he droned on as Ava realized he was rambling again and returned to her phone.

She decided to check to see if her latest posts had gotten any traction. With over three hundred followers she was starting to see some results, but she was ready to break onto the main feed. Her recent videos of a slow, sad version of the dances the other girls do had done pretty well, especially once she added in popular horror movie soundtracks as backing.

She suddenly felt a sharp pain in her right arm. When she pulled her arm away she could hear her brother snicker from behind her. He had pinched her! Retaliation was in order and she turned quickly to throw a small, and too short, arm towards her brother.

"Kids!" Dad admonished. "Knock it off you two, we're almost there."

"He keeps picking on me to look cool for his friend."

"Do not!" Jake insisted.

"That's enough. Ava, you sit and play your game. Jake, leave your sister alone."

Leave her alone?! Ava thought. *How about stop abusing your little sister for the entertainment of your weird friend? How about you're a horrible little goblin that would rather be a jerk than a big brother?*

Ava had been bored, now she was in a sour mood on top of that. Her dad had dragged them to L'Anse aux Meadows before. The site was the only confirmed Viking structure in North America, and therefore a place where people obsessed with history eventually end up. It also happened that her dad was a professor at a university that worked with the preservation society and got access when something new was discovered. The kids were collateral victims as their mother had a girls' weekend planned. She'd seen these lumps of grass before, she doubted that adding in a hole in the ground was going to make it more impressive.

The SUV rolled past the visitor's gate and headed towards the employee lot. After checking in they were sent to the nearby visitor center to meet with the staff member in charge, who they found waiting with an ATV.

"Dr. Tillmann?" the man asked.

"That's me," Dad answered. "Thanks for taking us out."

"Of course. Nice to meet you, I'm Mark. Happy to share the discovery with you, hopefully you can authenticate it."

"I hope so! More likely I'll take some info and pics, and if we're lucky some samples we can use to date the site. Was there any wood structure..."

Ava tuned out and looked at the vehicle. *Only four seats. I guess one of us is riding on the back. Maybe Bill can ride back there and fall off. That isn't fair, he's okay. Jake can fall off.*

"All right, let's load up," Mark said. "It's a four-seater, but the kids should be able to fit across the back."

"I can ride in the back!" Jake volunteered.

"Nah, sorry, bud. It's a bit of a drive and we can't have you falling off."
You just met him, you aren't qualified to make that decision.

As the smallest, Ava was designated to sit in the middle. As they started riding she noticed that the boys seemed to have plenty of room on the outside while she was unable to move her arms.

"Can you guys move to the edge?"

"Sorry, sis, don't want to get any dirt thrown up on my new sneakers."

"Yeah, plus we have to keep you snug and safe," Bill added.

I've changed my mind, he can ride on the back.

"How far away from the main site is it?" her dad was asking.

"About a kilometer inland. It's a bit out of the way from other artifacts we've found, and not near any game trails, which explains why we hadn't seen it before."

"How did you spot it if it's outside the park?"

"Not really outside the park, the site covers about 80 square kilometers. I was taking the buggy here out for observations, just checking that nothing is being disturbed or anything we need to worry about, and while I was driving past a small copse I heard some birds. When I stopped to get a look, I love birds, I thought I heard water and went to check it out."

"No one had thought to check that area for artifacts before?"

"We've uncovered thousands of artifacts in a site that best we can tell only operated a few years. Most study has been dedicated to either finding migration evidence to the south or spiraling out near the buildings to find more stuff. The tree growth is small, wasn't there when the Norse were so no one paid it any mind."

"Well, that's a good point. Wouldn't expect it to be this far out unless it was a natural spring they took advantage of. They may not have had what they needed to dig..."

"Did you just fart?!" Ava screamed.

"No! That was you," Jake replied.

The rest of the ride was thankfully short and consumed by sibling bickering and fatherly exasperation. As they neared the trees and the vehicle slowed down Ava looked at her phone and realized she wasn't getting any

6

signal out here. *Guess I'm stuck learning something. At least it's a nice day out.*

They stopped and got out before the trees and walked in so as to not disturb the site. As promised a quiet burbling of water soon came to their ears and led them to a small spring. As her father had hoped, there was some wood forming what may have been a structure around the spring that certainly hadn't gotten there naturally, despite the overgrowth.

"We had a geologist contact us and said it's probably a fracture spring," Mark said proudly.

"That right?" Dad said in that voice Ava knew was meant to convey he was listening even though he really wasn't.

As Dad went over to the site, stepping carefully around anything that looked mildly not like dirt he told the kids to hang back and not disturb the site. The boys started walking around the woods and finding sticks that would work for walking and / or sparring while Ava found a small rock to sit on. While she couldn't get service she decided to work on her own videos, recording them for editing and posting later. The sparse trees and rocks here would be a good backdrop for an ironically slow "Neon Trees—Animal" treatment. She put on her best unamused face and looked slightly up into the phone and began to recite the song.

"Here we go again," she mouthed a bit slower than the regular rhythm. "I feel the chemicals kicking in..."

"Hey, stinky! What are you doing? Filming some Kuhlr Talks? How's that coming by the way, got a big fan base yet?" Jake asked sarcastically, ruining her take.

"It's growing, unlike you."

"Dad said I'll have a late spurt! Why are you wasting your time, no one wants to watch a little girl pouting."

"Well, except other pouting little girls," Bill added.

"Leave me alone," Ava said, involuntarily letting a bit of emotion slip into her words and saw Jake's eyes focus. He smelled weakness from a mile away.

"Are you going to cry? I might watch that video. Spoiled kid realizes she's not special." He punctuated the supposed title with his hands, like reading it from a marquee.

"Shut up!" she tried to shout, but ended up little more than a squeak as she turned and walked a bit further into the trees.

"Let her go, you need to ease up on her," she heard Bill tell Jake as he began to pursue. She didn't hear Jake's reply if he had one, she had zagged around a few trees and could see that she had circled around the spring with her dad and Mark between her and where the boys were resuming their stick hunt. She sat behind a larger tree and composed herself, letting her tears stay on her cheeks.

Stupid Jake. I try to be nice to him, but he's always mean to me. I'm not spoiled! I can't help that I was born after dad got his job at the university and we were able to have nicer things when I was younger. That fact seemed to be something her 17-year-old brother held over her head when they argued. He'd talk about how she never had to struggle, though his definition of struggling seemed to be not having a phone until he was 10 and getting a TV in his room the same time she did.

As Ava glared at the rock in front of her, she noticed that the top of it seemed quite a bit flatter than the other rocks. It was small, maybe the size of a pancake, with some other rocks encircling it, though the circle had been broken long ago by roots that had overtaken the spot. She moved to have a look and noticed the rock had some grooves, but enough moss had grown in to make it unreadable.

Is this some kind of altar? From what dad has said the Norse that came over didn't bring any idols as far as they had found. Maybe just a marker telling people the well was here then? Not that they'd miss it, it's right over the rise there. Or just some stupid rocks and I'm trying to distract myself.

She decided to wipe the rock off the best she could and in a fit of inspiration decided that she could still get a video while she was out here. She checked to make sure her eyes were a little puffy, but not too obvious and started recording.

"I'm here at a lost Viking altar and taking a stand for the bullied little sisters everywhere," she said into the front-facing camera. She switched the scene to her dumping some of her candy onto the flat rock that now had a more believable "rune" shape showing and continued, "Hear me, gods of Valhalla, render punishment on those that harm innocents and protect those that are not jerks." As she panned towards her brother, now walking through the clearing towards her dad, she caught him trip and fall with some cartoonish flailing to the ground.

Omigod that's perfect! She thought as she ended the video on an obvious bouncing from laughter shot of Jake.

"I see you laughing!" he yelled towards her and got to his feet and started marching towards her.

"Jake, leave your sister alone," their dad called over his shoulder while gathering samples.

Jake ignored the distracted doctor and continued towards Ava. Bill jogged to catch up and walked briskly backwards in front of Jake trying to convince him to let it go. As they walked Ava started recording again, figuring evidence would be useful when they found her body.

"You don't get to laugh at me!" Jake said just loud enough for her to hear. "I've been nothing, but nice to you and AHH!"

In the middle of his monologue, a black bird flew down from the trees towards them. Bill slipped and stumbled backwards just as the bird got to them, which Jake hadn't seen, causing the bird to fly right in front of Jake's face. He whipped his arms up, forgetting the stick he was carrying which got caught in his backpack and sent him tumbling back down the hill again.

"KIDS! Get down here and behave yourselves," Dad shouted in his dad voice.

The kids all made their way down to the spring, their argument paused. Ava had stowed her phone, she got the video she needed and decided to leave it tucked away hoping Jake hadn't noticed or would forget she had filmed him. When their father had finished gathering his samples and taking measurements and pictures they loaded back into the vehicle and made their way to the Visitor's Center.

A dormant god slowly opened his eyes. He laid on his slab a bit, taking slow breaths and letting his mind focus.

Where am I? he wondered weakly. *Stone slab. Low light. Damp.*

He brought himself to a sitting position and stood briefly. Very briefly.

Argr. Legs weak, haven't been used in some time. Stone floor. Noise from ahead.

The newly awakened god began to crawl his way forward, eventually regaining enough strength to resume walking. He saw light through a door and attempted to quicken his pace. Upon reaching the door he could see a large hall with gleaming seats in a circle. There were voices that he couldn't make out coming from shapes he had trouble seeing through the gleam of the marble floors and the crack he was peering through. Seeing no latch, he pushed the door open.

As the door swung it creaked on old hinges that echoed through the room. The voices cut off sharply and he saw the shapes go rigid. Hurried whispers carried from between the seats.

"Did that come from..."

"That can only mean..."

"Who?"

From around the largest of the seats a man stepped, looking at the god with one eye.

"Welcome back child. Take it easy, you haven't regained your strength yet."

Odin. The name leapt to his mind as if a faraway echo.

"Where am I? What happened?" He coughed through dry lips.

"You're in Asgard, at Gladsheim. You've just come from the crypt where we put the Forgotten."

"The Forgotten?"

"Yes. Those who no longer have worshippers and have passed on from the memory of man. Now think, do you know who you are?"

"I... I don't."

"I feared as much. It happens. Does anyone recognize this returned brother?" Odin asked the other figures who were peering through the seats. The god realized only a handful were there.

"I believe I do," a voice carried from the seat Odin had occupied.

"Uncle? You know him?" Odin asked as he returned and fetched a living head to bring closer. *Mimir.* The echo in his mind recalled.

"Well, he's a bit ragged, but I remember. A test should confirm. Hear me son? Before you came from the crypt, Odin and Freyja here were debating the fate of the man that stands behind these onlookers. He died in glorious battle, and by rights, Freyja and Odin each receive half of those that die in battle. Now, we don't get many souls here these days, fewer battles and even fewer of those who worship us that die in them. Neither has had a new soul in some time. Look on him and tell me who you believe should have the claim."

A woman walked forward with a man in a uniform. She appeared frail, but her steps betrayed strength and her eyes reflected the forest even here.

Freyja.

She brought the man before him and stepped back to stand beside Odin, looking questioningly at Mimir. The forgotten god gazed upon the man, a stranger wearing strange clothes and a strange hairstyle. He examined the man, noticing an image of Mjölnir inked to the man's arm. He found his mind clearing as he searched the man, not knowing how he was to choose this man's fate.

"Valhalla or Folkvang?" Mimir asked.

He gazed into the man's eyes and, as if through an old memory, knew that the man was brave, had aspired to military service and died protecting his fellow warriors. He had aspired to Valhalla, muttering the word even as he died clutching his weapon. He felt his fear, his excitement, and his regrets. He had left behind a wife and child.

"By tradition," he rasped, not knowing what he was saying, but feeling as if he were being controlled by another, "Freyja chooses half of those who die each day in battle, and the other half are given to Odin. If Freyja deems this warrior worthy of the fields then let the Valkyries carry him off, and Odin will have claim to the next to pass through this hall."

As he finished his judgement a swirl of black feathers blew through the room and the warrior was gone. The gods came closer now, and he knew now that these were all gods.

"I believe that answers the question," Mimir said. "Welcome back, Forseti."

A sharp inhale of breath came from among the assembled gods, though he didn't know from whom. He knew Mimir was right though, he was Forseti. He knew that he was a god, and that one of the seats here belonged to him, though beyond that the details eluded him still. Odin's eye clouded as if he were searching his mind for the name.

"Of course," exclaimed Odin. "Son of Balder, we are glad to see you again. Will you sit?"

"I will. Can you show me to my seat? Can you explain what's happened?"

Odin walked Forseti to one of the chairs, thrones really. This one was dusty from disuse and appeared to be made of silver and gold, dulled by time.

"It's been nearly a thousand years since you last walked this hall," Mimir began. "Around that time nearly all of us became weaker and eventually fell asleep. Those who worshiped us had died out, and their descendants adopted the beliefs of the lands they traveled to or of the Christians that were spreading through our lands. You remember the Christians?"

Forseti nodded, they were gaining traction and being spread by the Romans during his time.

"They're still around. We, on the other hand, were doomed to obscurity it seemed. With no one to send us offerings or keep us energized by their thoughts we slumbered. Sometime later writings of us resurfaced and were studied by scholars. Our stories started to be told again, though as myth. These stories woke some, such as Odin, Thor, and Loki. While they regained strength they moved those of us that slumbered to the crypt and left the door unbarred so as we awoke we could come to join the others. Well, some of us. Frey was awake and calling out for days before Tyr finally heard him. Recently, as these stories have spread and our names become further known we've gained strength. It seems as though your story has made it to one of man's entertainments, too."

"Entertainments?" Forseti scoffed.

"Indeed. Much has changed and much of our strength now draws from games the humans play, or plays they act out. It isn't as powerful as worship or offerings, but a small amount of thought from millions of people will bring strength."

"How many is millions?"

"More than all those who worshiped us in the past combined. There will be time for that soon enough. For now, you should go and rest, gather your strength."

"My hall? Does it still stand?"

"It does," one of the goddesses nearby interrupted. "I will take you there, grandson."

Frigg

As the pair walked from the hall the remaining gods watched after them. Odin, Mimir, Tyr, Freyja, Frey, and Bragi remained silent until they were out of sight.

"Tyr, figure out what woke him," Odin said steadily.

"I will."

"Bragi, go find Loki and bring him to me."

"Yes, Father."

Frigg walked Forseti to the door of a great hall. The hall had once been beautiful, but now stood open and unused, the gold columns and silver roof no longer shining. He stepped through the entryway and walked among the rubble to his throne. Frigg held his arm as they walked, and brushed away the dirt on the throne so he could sit.

"Why was I Forgotten so long?" he asked.

"I do not know. Some still slumber, but the other Aesir rose long ago. Some are still weak, and a few have returned to the crypt, Forgotten again. We thrive on the whims of those in Midgard, and they have short memories."

"I must rest, I find myself overwhelmed."

"Of course, child. Rest here, no harm will come to you. When you are of strength, return to the hall."

"My mother and father?"

"Balder remains weak, but can be found on his ship Hringhorni. I'm afraid Nanna hasn't been seen in some time, I believe she remains Forgotten."

As Frigg walked out, Forseti gazed after her. He noticed that she was quicker to leave than she had been bringing him here.

You're imagining things. You've slumbered a thousand years and returned to a world you know little of. Millions? How are gods forgotten? If our worshipers had been subjugated the conquerors would burn our altars and have slain our priests. If some of us have risen, then writings endured. If the writings endured, why would I remain uncelebrated?

Forseti stared into the broken pieces of his home and soon fell asleep, exhausted.

3

Forseti opened his eyes again, taking in the crumbling hall around him and a moment to gather his memories. He remembered being plagued with questions the night before, but unable to grasp them as if through a fog.

Someone should have answers. Rather, maybe someone should have the questions since I don't seem to.

Forseti rose from his throne, thinking himself a bit taller and stronger than he had been. He disregarded that as being more well rested and began walking back towards the hall in which he had last seen the gods. Upon entry he noticed the hall was empty save a few other frail people milling about, the thrones abandoned. Forseti made his way towards the people he saw.

"Excuse me, do you know where Odin and the others are?"

After bewildered looks and a few grunts, he decided to leave them alone and continued to look around. Walking the line of thrones, he noticed Mimir resting at the foot of Odin's seat.

"Mimir? Where have the Aesir gone?"

"To converse I believe. Not sure where, they left me here to watch over things—even if they didn't leave me the best viewing spot."

"They're having a conversation without their greatest counsel?" Forseti asked as he picked up Mimir and sat him on the arm of Odin's throne.

"I must assume they aren't discussing matters needing counsel, otherwise I would have the same question. What brings you here, Forseti? I'm glad to see you're on your feet and have some wits about you."

"Yes, thanks. I'm not sure. I have a lot of questions, but am unsure what those queries are, really."

"Ah. Does it feel a bit like a fog after too much libation? Like there is something just out of reach?"

"Yes! It frustrates me."

"It happens to all who awake, and I suspect the longer you were asleep causes the feeling to compound. I call it 'The Fog'."

"Why do I feel like I have competing memories? My parents, you... It all feels wrong."

"Interesting. Many have doubts, but I haven't known any to be able to reconcile them. I suspect you're awakening faster than *The Fog* can do its job. Whatever happened to bring you back is certainly popular."

"What..." Forseti began as Mimir cut him off.

"Rest child, I'll explain what I can. You always were wiser than most so no sense honey-coating. Your mind is reconciling what your reality was when you were last awake and what the reality has become since. As the Aesir and Vanir began going to sleep it occurred to me that we were sustained by the belief of the humans. Odin took me to my well and I dedicated much time to understanding our nature. We exist because they believe we do. In the absence of knowledge, they ascribed godly intervention to natural phenomena. I was able to see other realities, the Greeks, the Romans, the Christians—all with their own gods and stories. I even saw you, Forseti, as you were formed. A Greek god of the sea that became a god to the Germanics and Frisians as their cultures integrated, eventually becoming the one who presides over disputes here in Asgard. My memory too, was at odds, for I remembered you always being here, but the well showed me that it wasn't so. You keeping up so far?"

"I think so. We're imaginary?"

"No, we're quite real. I'm not sure how we got that way, or why. That's unimportant for now, back to you. Your memories are now being updated with the beliefs about you since you were last around. A thousand years is a long time and in that period our stories have changed. You, for example, went from a lone god that walked out of the sea to being the child of Balder and Nanna because a Lawspeaker, one of yours, said so many years after our downfall. I've been awake all this time, sustained by no more than my name being known. Only being a head has its advantages for energy conservation. I've changed too, thanks to popular depictions of me! Can you remember what I looked like before, I wonder?"

Hanging from Odin's belt, a head with dried organs hanging from the neck. The head was mummified, no signs of life, but still covered in herbs. Odin would pull it to his ear at times.

"I... I do." Forseti claimed, then held his head in his hands as a wave of nausea washed over him.

"Interesting, indeed. When I've challenged others the pain broke their concentration and their new reality quickly supplanted their old memories. You are gaining strength fast enough to fight it. Those who wander behind you, many have been awake for a hundred years and lack the strength to recall their own names yet, you've been back merely a day. I do think I look a bit better though. You should see Thor and Hel! Talk about a make-over."

"So, I understand what you're saying. What happened though? Why were we forgotten?"

"The Christians won, as I explained when you awoke. They forced our people to listen to their beliefs, but the Norse are strong willed and resisted for many years.

"When the Christians began to explain that we were really the same though, gave them just enough to justify it to themselves, we were done. 'Valhalla? Of course we have that, but you don't need to die in glorious battle, just believe!' and 'Oh you have an afterlife ruled by Hel? That's interesting, ours is Hell, too, and it's only for the bad people that don't believe in our unimaginatively named god and it's all torture, all the time.'

"Our stories, our celebrations, integrated into their beliefs and our people integrated soon after. A few texts remained, mostly written years later from the oral record and put into a neat story that didn't really match with the rough collection of deities we really were. They got close on a lot though."

"You sound bitter."

"I am. A thousand years watching our story change and become sanitized for audiences all while those around me are unable to grasp the atrocity. I can remember hundreds of Aesir, Vanir, and Giants who have yet to rise and likely never will as no writings of their deeds exist."

"I'm Greek?"

"Kind of. The Greek you still exists, quite a bit more well-known I may add. Anyway, stay focused. It took many years for Odin and the others to regain their strength. You though, you walked out of the crypt of your own power yesterday and today have walked back in here even stronger and more alert. I don't know what has transpired, but my guess is that you're getting more than just your name in a play. I recommend you go back to your home, focus your mind and remember how to observe Midgard. Find those who are strengthening you and understand your path."

"Thank you, Mimir. I'd say you've always been good to me, but I don't know if that's true."

"Truth is a funny thing," Mimir said as Forseti placed him at the foot of Odin's throne and left the hall.

Forseti returned home and took his place on his throne, taking a few moments to sweep aside the rubble from the dais. As he sat he looked around again and thought that perhaps the walls seemed a bit less dusty than they had the day before.

Observe the mortals? How did I do that? Not sure how I feel about what Mimir has told me, the mortals giving life and strength to the immortals. They're so short-lived and... inconsequential. We'd watch them on their sailings or battles to be entertained, cheering on our favored warriors. I remember one battle in Brunanburh, I watched it with a few others over... there!

Hurrying over to a low, flat table he set to wiping it clean, revealing a silver surface polished to a mirror finish. A gift from Tyr officially, he really gave it so he could decide battles while they drank together. The mirror charged a price, one that hadn't been a concern before—essence of an Aesir's divinity. Delivered in the form of blood it extracted the power of a god, what Forseti now assumed was given by the belief and offerings of the mortals.

He wasn't sure how much strength he had to spare, but he needed to know what had happened in the time he slept, and who now was giving entertainment or offerings in his name. Dragging his hand along a cracked bit of marble, he dripped the blood on the mirror, spreading it around the glass and focusing on finding the one to whom he owed his reawakening. As the image began to resolve he saw trees, grass, and a massive building.

This is the largest longhouse I've ever seen, what king rules from here?

As the image came closer he saw many people coming into the building, smaller people mostly. *Children?* He noticed the carriages they emerged from, and their lack of horses. While he didn't understand all he saw, he knew that enough time had passed for large changes and he would find more later if he had the energy. He could feel himself becoming tired already so continued to search for his summoner.

As he moved into the school, he realized the extent of the changes to the building style, and the exceptional number of children. There were adults, dressed strangely, but obviously commanding the children. He noticed a glow down a corridor and moved towards the energy. As he approached he saw that the glow surrounded a small female child. He had seen this glow before, it indicated that this person was a source of a request for Forseti's intervention, and that they had paid a price for the service. He stared skeptically at this girl, until he saw a symbol of his on the papers she was holding.

17

The oarless boat and my axe. This dark haired child called on me, and returned me from my slumber? Glancing around the halls he looked closer at the crowd. They moved through and around his view, all in similar clothing. Many of the children, and a few of the adults, had dim auras indicating they had partaken in a celebration of Forseti. He understood this and with thought determined that the strength of the glow likely showed how much energy they had given to the one watching, a connection across the realms that would fade in time. Ava shone like a beacon among the dimmer lights.

She spread my story. They participated in that which she produced, and their attention gave me strength. Looking back towards the girl he saw that others were approaching her, each glowing brighter than those in the sea of faces, though none as bright as the girl.

"Ava!" One of the girls shouted. "I totally tried your altar thing..." Forseti heard before he started to drift away. He was feeling tired and weak, his power was draining and he was losing focus in the mirror.

Ava. An altar. This... child... was his gyðja? Priestess, that's the word for it in her language. Good to know. The others, followers of Ava?

As his view backed from the building and back into the sky he swore to hear their requests and protect them, these odd children who had called to him in their despair, apparently in their military training facility.

"Hear me gods of Valhalla, render judgement on those that harm innocents and protect those that are not jerks."

Ava had watched the video of her brother tumbling a dozen times while she edited it down to make it fit with the music, and a few more times while she added cartoon fall noises, then took those out to keep the integrity of the moment. She was finally happy with her edit and hit publish, then immediately sending it to her school friends on Kuhlr. She waited impatiently for them to watch it and send her validation that it was indeed a masterpiece of drama and comedy.

Ding. "LOL."

Ding. "Phhbbtt, is that Jake? Good!"

Ding, Ding, Ding.

This was the best response she had gotten yet on her videos, and she smiled smugly as she put her phone away to go down for dinner.

"So, tell me about the trip. Was the well authentic?" Mom asked as Dad brought the pizza in. They had just gotten home a few hours earlier and Judi Tillmann was getting home from work, pizza was the obvious solution to everyone's tired condition.

"I'm quite sure it is!" Dad replied "I'm not sure what it'll get me for funding or tourists, it's a bit out of the way from the main site and isn't overly impressive from a layman's perspective. I think it'll be more exciting for researchers and historians."

"Well, that's something! And you authenticated it, that has to be good for an entry in a book, right?"

"Maybe a wiki if I'm lucky. We knew there was a well somewhere, we just finally found it."

"You undersell yourself. How about you guys? Did you have a good trip?"

"It was fine." Jake answered quickly. "Bill and I made a sea shanty to celebrate the discovery."

"Nope." Dad cut him off. In response to his wife's inquiring look he responded, "I overheard them working on it in the backseat. Unless you want a dirge on how Vikings went about choosing their holes and how much liquid they could produce you're better off."

"Ew. Jake!"

Jake shrugged at his mom and tried to hold in a chuckle. "What? Don't stifle my creativity."

"And Ava, were you less of a deviant than these *boys*?"

"I didn't play with the hole as much as they did. The first time Jake saw it he fell over in shock."

"Did not, it was slippery down there!"

"That's what she... nope. Not giving in," Mom corrected herself. "Go ahead, Ava."

"I mostly talked with friends and took pictures, it was real pretty on the coast, I got a couple cool pics at the recreation site with the actors."

They chatted a bit more and cleaned up their pizza before heading to their areas again. Mom and Dad went to the living room to watch TV, and the kids each returned to their rooms.

"Jake, don't forget the trash," Mom shouted up the steps after them.

"Ugh. Okay."

Ava gave him a quick mocking *haha*, to which Jake responded by shoulder checking her into her door.

Jerk. Mom definitely heard him bump me, why isn't she doing anything about it? She saw more messages coming in responding to the video. She wondered if she could make her own altar, if the others were digging that vid, maybe she can work on a sequel. After copying the shape on the stone to a piece of paper she grabbed a piece of candy from her stash under the bed and started recording.

"Oh nameless god, I am asking you again for your divine justice. Strike down those who persecute the weak!"

Now I'll hold that clip and wait until I can catch him doing something stupid. She heard him drag the trash bins to the curb and Dad let him know he had missed one. As he marched back for the bag she began recording, figuring the only way to get the footage was to record and delete if nothing happened.

She ended up not waiting long. As Jake came through the gate he snagged the bag on a piece of fence and Ava could see liquid starting to run onto the driveway. As Jake walked he glanced down and saw the mystery liquid getting onto his shoes. With a sneer he held the bag out further, the change in grip causing the bag to hit the ground as he picked up pace towards the can. As Jake reached the curb, he bent his arm to raise the bag up quickly, and as he began to lift it the hole plus the ground trauma proved too much for the material, splitting open and dumping used napkins and pizza boxes onto the yard. Jake slumped his shoulders and looked to the sky in resignation.

And cut! Holy crap, that's awesome. I need to edit and send this ASAP! No, wait. I need to give it a few days and work the algorithm. What are the odds?

She went back to her messages and Kuhlr comments to see if anyone new had watched it. She spent the rest of the night scrolling and checking her notifications.

〜 〜 〜

Forseti awakened feeling better rested. He investigated his palace and surveyed what was left of his former home. As he stood and began to walk, he felt strength returning to his legs. Stopping at the bottom of the dais he turned his mind inward, listening to the voice straining to return his memories.

They would stand here and plead their cases. I would sit in judgement and hear their pleas. All of them, the immortals, this is where they would come to settle disputes. I remember squabbles between the seven daughters of Ran and Aegir over who needed to take care of Heimdall while the others took a trip, Sif and Jarnsaxa arguing over Thor's indiscretions, Loki and Tyr battling about... something. It was hard to keep track of all the times the Giant was dragged before him.

He continued his walk among the pillars, running his fingers through the dust building on them. Beneath he could see gold, shining like a mirror in the sun.

Glitnir. The one who shines. These golden columns and silver roof could be seen all across the realm, a symbol of debate and discussion in a society of strength and action. What's become of you? Of me? Of all of us? Odin seemed healthy compared to my own state, but he was still a shadow of himself and the Great Hall was in a way I've never seen. Forgotten?

As he made his way to the edge of the hall he saw long tables where banquets had been held, where audiences would gather for hearings. There were lower pillars here that had held vases and trophies that now sat empty.

Those bastards! Where's my stuff? A guy falls asleep for a while and his palace gets ransacked? There was a vase celebrating my horseracing victory against Hel and Sleipnir here. I beat an 8 legged horse, I earned that. To be fair the 8 legs got a bit tangled up so it wasn't a fair race, but still! Where's the harp I got from Bragi after judging his singing competition? And over here there was a spear made of... Mistletoe.

A feeling of swelling racked Forseti's head, as if his mind was rearranging itself to accommodate new information. He was driven to his knees by the pressure and behind his closed eyes he saw the death of Balder. Balder, invincible and beautiful, had been so beloved that every object in the realms had promised to not hurt him, except the young and fragile mistletoe. The spear was thrown by Balder's own blind brother as the gods took turns throwing things at Balder knowing he could not be hurt. Balder died, his brother was killed for his actions.

Wait. Why did Frigg say Balder and Nanna were my parents? Why did I ask about my parents? I don't remember having parents. But, I do remember them being my parents. How's he alive and on his boat when he died and was burnt on it?

The pressure continued to build in his head and he was forced to abandon his thoughts to retire to his bedchamber. Upon seeing the chamber similarly ruined and the soft materials destroyed he decided to return to his throne to rest longer.

5

"Ava! I totally tried your altar thing. The weird post man that's always looking at me shut his finger in the box today," Shellie said as she ran up to her in the hall.

"Really? You tried the symbol?" Ava laughed.

"Yeah! Mom went by the community post on the way in and I had already drawn it in my notebook so when I saw him I put a piece of scone on the notebook and made an offering. Next thing I know he goes to shut the back of the box while looking towards me and jumps back shaking his hand. I wish I had recorded it..."

"I recorded one, but it wasn't as funny," Alison said. "I put some cashews on the symbol and asked for my stupid dog to fall down the steps."

"Allie!" Ava and Shellie interjected.

"Not the whole way, just a couple of steps so he'd stop coming up to my room maybe!"

"I hope it didn't work." Ava said with a bit of red in her cheeks

"No, the dog just pooped in my doorway and wandered off..."

"Good. Maybe the Unknown God is a pet lover."

"Or has a nut allergy," Shellie added helpfully. "Unknown God, is that what we're going with?"

"I don't know who he or she is."

"Fair. Your video is starting to take off, it had over three hundred views last I looked."

"I know, I have a second video I'm going to post at 2:00 from Science class. I read that's the best time to post a Kuhlr that you want to get a lot of views because of when school ends or something."

The bell rang and the girls ran off to their class at the end of the hall. During the class, Ava noticed the symbols for the Unknown God on the notebooks of both of her friends and she smirked, drawing it on the back of her own as well.

You never know when you'll need a quick retribution video.

"You shouldn't have put that video out about your brother," Samantha whispered to her while the teacher distributed handouts. Ava rolled her eyes, mentally anyway. Samantha was Ava's friend as well, but she had a weird crush on Jake ever since he helped her after she went too deep in the pool.

"It's just a joke. He'll be okay."

"Has he seen it? Did he agree to it?"

"I didn't agree to getting bullied or going to Nowhereville, Newfoundland either. We all find the strength to endure." Ava made an exaggerated *What's this loon on about?* face to Alison when she turned her attention back to her desk.

Apparently the vocalized acknowledgement of the video was the opening needed. A boy behind her, Seth, leaned forward. "Does that make you his priestess?"

"I prefer to think of them as a She. And maybe! Teaching the gospel of punishing jerks."

"Ava, have you already grown bored with our mitochondria lesson?" the teacher said from behind, er... in front of her.

"Umm... no, sir! I was just telling Seth how excited I was for this powerhouse of a lesson."

The room giggled, somehow even without the lesson yet everyone knew that factoid. Their teacher took advantage of the segue and launched into his lecture. Ava glanced around. It hadn't occurred to her that the nameless viewers of her vids might be people that she actually knew.

Now she was a bit anxious about putting the next one up and it was almost the prime time to publish. While her teacher's back was turned she pulled her phone out, opened the Kuhlr app and accessed her draft vids. She had already prepped this one with commentary so all she needed to do was hit the publish button and vids of Jake getting a trash shower would be everywhere.

"Ava!"

"Yes sir?!" Ava jumped as she hit the home button on her phone.

"What is so important? You know there's no phones allowed in class."

"Sorry, my dog isn't feeling well, and my mom was taking him to the vet today. I was checking to see if she had any news yet."

"I see, class will be over in a few minutes. I hope your dog is okay, but please pay attention."

Ava nodded and slipped her phone back into her pocket until the bell rang. As she sat on the bus she went back into the app and realized she had uploaded the video when she thought she hit the home button.

Oh, good. I have some notifications. Holy shi...

"Holy shit!" Shellie said from beside her, gaping at her own phone. "Ava, you're viral!"

"It's not that big a deal, it's just a few thousand."

"Ava, you were on my front page as soon as I opened the app. You made front page!"

"Really?" Ava released a squeal that scared bats for miles around and drew glares from all over the bus. She rode home in excitement and hurried talks with her friends. They debated on if the second video would do as well and if she should pin this video for future fans. As she got off the bus smiling she saw Jake standing across the street glaring at her.

Uh oh. I'm guessing he saw it. DID SAMANTHA TELL HIM?!

"You think that's funny? You made me look bad to the whole world!"

"Technically, you did that, I just documented it. I'm a journalist."

"I'm telling Dad."

"Come on, Jake, I didn't mean it to be seen by that many people."

"Then take it down!"

"Ha. No."

Jake took off towards the house. Ava assumed that the witnesses walking the neighborhood had kept her from being buried alive. She waved and nodded thankfully towards the old lady across the street on her porch. When she got inside she found her dad watching Jake's phone with Jake standing behind him with a wicked grin.

"Ava, why..." her dad started.

"I didn't think it would go viral!" she began to protest

"No, honey. Why didn't you tell me about the icon you found?"

"What?" the kids both answered in decidedly different tones.

"Well, I mean, ummm... You shouldn't have posted that video of Jake so you'll be grounded for that, but where was this? Was this at the well site?"

"Uhh, yeah. It was up the hill a bit from where you were working."

"We have to go, now!" her dad said as he began gathering his briefcase.

"What?"

"Come on, hopefully no one else has found it yet."

As his eyes opened, Forseti realized he felt quite well rested. Taking a few tentative steps at first, and then faster steps and even a bit of bouncing, he couldn't help but smile.

I thought I pushed it too far with the viewing mirror and would need more time to recover. The small one's work is taking seed, giving me energy.

He looked into a mirrored column, seeing his clothes fitting more normally and looking a bit less time worn. His complexion had less marks and hair was becoming fuller. Forseti nodded approvingly before attempting a few poses to see if his muscle mass had made a return as well. It had not.

Ah, well. My legs feel strong still, perhaps a walk around Asgard would be enjoyable. I'm still not sure who's here and who isn't, or what's become of our home.

Turning the opposite way of Odin's Gladsheim and heading down the row of mansions, Forseti let his mind wander, trying to recall who his neighbors had been. Next door was Landvidi, the home of Vidar. Once a thriving jungle of vines and foliage that were shaped into a house, it now sat empty. The branches bore no leaves or flowers and patches of light shone through the gaps in the wood. Across the large street sits Ydalir, the home of Ullr. This land is filled with yew trees stretching for miles, which Ullr would use to make intricate bows. The overrun land now seemed to indicate Ullr was not in residence, or perhaps too weak to chop the trees. After walking past the large properties, Breithablik came into view.

Balder's hall. It seems in better condition, but I was told Balder is living on his ship now. If he is awake perhaps he will be able to speak with me.

Forseti continued past the broad palace and turned to head for the water. On the hill in the distance he saw Himinbjorg, the home of Heimdall and the connection to the Bifrost. As he neared the water he came to Noatun, Njorth's home where travelers rest and ask for success in their fishing endeavors. Hringhorni, the most perfect ship ever built, was docked nearby.

"Over here!" A voice called out from the dock of Njorth's home. "Come and have a drink with us!" As Forseti approached the voice he saw two figures. One was identifiable as Njorth while the other had his back to him. When the seated man turned around Forseti was struck by his beauty.

"Balder! I was just coming to find you." Forseti said breathlessly as he hurried to the dock.

"Hello, son!" Balder said. Looking closer Forseti could see the man wasn't as healthy as he once was, his face was thin and hair streaked with grey. While still the most handsome being Forseti had seen since his return, he was a pale reminder of the radiance of Balder past. "I had heard you awoke, one of Odin's crows told us in exchange for some fish."

"But you didn't come to see me?"

"I've been awake for a while, but lack the strength to make any journey. I awoke on my boat, docked just there, and had only the power to come to Njorth's house from time to time. Thor stopped by once and took Nanna with him to Gladsheim, where he said the rest of the Forgotten rest. Njorth here woke a bit before I did, and his stocks of ale were still full. Would you like a drink?"

"Yes, thank you," Forseti answered as he took a seat on a nearby log. "How are you here though? The last I saw you, you were being burned on that ship along with Nanna, your horse, and a dwarf.

"Don't forget Draupnir!" Balder said over his mug, referring to Odin's ring that was said to drip eight new golden rings every nine days. "Nearly drowned in the rings when I woke up, luckily one of the windows was open and the rings had been spilling out into the sea. I'm not sure why I'm back, to answer your question. I remember being struck by a spear and feeling pain for the first time, then I was awake and weakened with my wife asleep at my side and unable to be woken. Thor says a thousand years have passed."

"Yes. I've looked on the world. It is quite different from when we last visited there. Our fates and strength are tied to the adoration of the Midgardians, and they have started to remember and recite our stories. As stories are told more are brought back."

"How is my story told but not of your mother?"

"I don't know. I don't really remember her being my mother though, that's part of the changes. Do you remember her well?"

"Of course! I observed her bathing in the forest and was struck by her

27

beauty. I asked her father for her hand, but had to do combat with her other suitor to win her hand."

"Yes, and who was this suitor?"

"Hoth."

"Your blind brother?"

"No... wait. It was a different Hoth."

"Was it? How did you die?"

"Hoth threw a spear of mistletoe at me."

"Why was Nanna so distraught over your death that she died, when she really wanted to marry the other Hoth in the first place."

"She came to adore me, even coming to Hel to find me and try to bring me back."

"Didn't you give Draupnir to someone to return to Odin when they came to Hel?"

"Hermod, yes."

"How do you still have it?"

"I... I'm not sure. My head begins to ache."

"Alas. That's your mind rectifying the stories that have been told in the past thousand years. Soon it'll pass and you will remember only what the most powerful belief is, I think. I should let you rest."

"Forseti?" Njorth asked.

"Yes?"

"You are said to be the wisest in judgement, and you seem quite healthier than many of the gods that are now awake. I'm wondering if you could solve a debate between Balder and I?"

"Oh come now Njorth, still you must rub this in?" Balder complained.

"What is it?" Forseti asked.

"A contest. As you no doubt remember, my wife Skadi chose me as her husband when Odin made her choose based on our feet. Skadi chose my feet as most beautiful and Balder here has been upset ever since."

"How can she see your feet as more beautiful!?"

"I thought you lusted after none other than Nanna?" Forseti asked Balder.

"Ouch, my head."

"So will you judge our feet, Forseti?" Njorth pleaded. "Put this question to sleep for good."

"I can, show me your feet."

"Should we be behind a curtain or hidden?"

"I am the god of fair judgement, I will not be influenced by whom the feet are attached."

The gods presented their feet on the table between them and Forseti began examining them. After a few walks around and a poke here and there he was ready to render his judgement.

"I declare Balder's feet the most beautiful, though Njorth does have amazingly fair feet for a fisherman."

"Ha, I knew it!" Balder laughed as his feet glowed a bit and became smoother. Njorth's feet glowed as well, now showing yellow in his toenails.

"No wonder they erased you..." Njorth grumbled.

"What was that?" Forseti asked quickly.

"Nothing! Just complaining about my loss is all. Said no wonder the Midgardians forgot about you, their god of feet. Just a jest!"

"Ah. Haha. Yes, I see." Forseti said. His smile didn't reach his eyes though, instead he was focused on Njorth who withered a bit under his gaze.

"Son, go and ask after dear Nanna, if she awakens please have her brought to me so I can see her again. If I'm ever of the strength I will come to visit you at your hall, perhaps stay there like in old times."

"Yes... father. As in the old times. I lack the strength to carry you now, stay here and drink your ale. I will return for you when I am able." Forseti finished his mug, bid farewell to the Aesir and the Vanir and began to walk away.

"Wait!" Njorth called. "Tell me, are my children awake? What news of them?"

"I saw Freyja and Frey just a bit ago. They are awake and doing well, though neither as strong as they once were. Should I send them word from you?"

"Please, tell them I am here and besotted by this drunken fool with such great feet. Perhaps they can find it in their schedules to visit their dear father."

"I will."

Forseti set off to climb the path back to Glitnir, Njorth's words echoing in his mind.

Erased.

After 30 minutes of calls to her mom, to his department chair at Dalhousie University, and the charter airline, Ava found herself and her brother in a car on the way to the airport. On the plane, Dr. Harrison Tillmann watched the video and analyzed each frame, asking Ava for any other vids or pics she had of it. He was referencing the symbol against his notes from his laptop, eventually superimposing the video frame over vases and other artifacts. He talked so animatedly about the possibility of finding a real altar that even Jake forgot the indignity of his place in the video and was getting excited.

"That looks like an axe, it's a shrine to Thor!" Jake exclaimed.

"Quiet down." Dad hushed him looking around suspiciously. The other pensioners on the flight weren't likely to steal their discovery, but one couldn't be too careful. "Plus, I don't think so. Thor is associated with Mjölnir almost exclusively. The axe was just in that comic movie. Besides, this is a double-bladed axe. And this part here doesn't make sense. It looks like a boat maybe."

"Is the axe the sail from the boat, maybe?" Ava asked, hoping everyone had forgotten she showed tens of thousands of people and counting a vid of her brother looking stupid.

"I doubt it, it isn't connected and this is looking down at the ship, not from the side."

"You sure it's a boat? It looks kind of like a... well, you know." Jake whispered.

"Don't finish that thought Jacob." Dad warned. He turned his head a bit and looked at the pic anew though. "Also, no it doesn't. What kind of videos... you know what, never mind."

Once they had loaded into the car Ava took the back seat and caught up on her notifications and messages with her friends. Her vid continued to grow and she was noticing that people had started using her audio or tagging "Unknown

God" to their videos, emulating her. She began putting a new video together, stitching video of the passing landscape with Led Zeppelin's *Immigrant Song*.

Valhalla, I am coming
On we sweep with threshing oar
Our only goal will be the western shore

She added a note to the video that she was on her way to the "OG altar" to verify it is real and who the Unknown God really is, so stay tuned! She was quite sure this would only exist a short time in the Kuhlr cycle, but she was going to milk it for all the followers, and maybe sponsors, she could get. She uploaded it, trusting that the popularity of the sound would bring people to find her.

When they reached the visitors center they again encountered Mark.

"Hey, gang! Dr. Tillmann, we have the UTV ready to go and the University contacted us already to expect news centers to call or set up video conferences so we've set up a studio area at the front desk."

"Dal thinks the media will be interested?"

"Not Dalhousie, King's College."

"Really? Interesting."

They were loaded into the vehicle and on their way before the conversation had a chance to get any more boring.

"Has anyone disturbed the site?"

"No sir! We didn't know what was really going on until they called and sent us the video about an hour ago. Haven't had time to go look at it ourselves."

The University of King's College sent a video I made to a Canadian Historical Site to inform them of a landmark discovery? What is my life right now?

Upon arrival at the site they had Ava lead them to the spot and began taking pictures and samples. They were able to assume that the circle had been complete before the trees grew in and based on where they think the villagers accessed the spring they determined the icon would have been out of view of most visitors, which Dad mentioned would have likely been necessary for it to remain. After thoroughly documenting it, her dad went about cleaning it very meticulously. Ava reminded him that she wiped it off with her hand a few days ago.

"Yes, but if I did that I would have to turn in my degree."

Once clean the symbol stood out sharply, a top down view of a boat with no oars and above that a 2-headed axe.

"Beautiful... This is amazing!" Dad said breathlessly. "There has never been a shrine to this god. The only other one we know of was defiled and renamed by a Christian missionary around 700 CE."

As they returned to the UTV her dad continued to mutter to himself and rationalize his assumptions. Upon reaching the visitors center they were shown inside and greeted by a young lady at the desk who informed them they had missed more calls than she remembers the site getting in the past month and handed over her notes.

"Seems the University really wants to talk," Dr. Tillmann began before the phone resumed ringing. "I'll get it if that's okay." The girl nodded. "Hello? Yes, it's me... Uh huh. Uh huh... I understand. Well, I don't know for sure I would need to confer with... really? HOW MANY?! They want to interview when? NOW?!"

The one-sided conversation of surprise and panic lasted another couple of minutes before Dad hung up and called the group together.

"Okay, we have a video interview in about five minutes with a few news outlets. We'll have to use my laptop. Mark, do you have some speakers or a microphone we can use? Great. Ava some of the outlets have requested you to be there too so I'll announce the discovery officially and answer a few questions before bringing you in. Seems your video has attracted a lot of attention, including from other mythology buffs that figured out who's altar it was and Dal wants to get the official announcement out before any of them get picked up. Luckily since hardly anyone knew about the well they haven't put together where we found the mark yet, most are just assuming it was a prop you made and flexing their obscure god knowledge."

Ava had been caught up in the moment since getting to the spot and had forgotten about her video. She pulled her phone out and saw the screen overflowing with notifications, mostly from Kuhlr, but also messages from her friends, her mom, and other social apps where classmates were connected with her. She was going to message her mom first but heard her dad on the phone with her so she moved to Kuhlr.

The video is at over 400 THOUSAND VIEWS?! 57,000 new followers, 38,000 comments between the 3 videos and even a few people creeping into her older vids and commenting. What?! Calm down, deep breaths, it's okay... Wait, did he say I'm going to be interviewed by news companies?

Before Ava could dwell on it too long her dad was beginning his call and Mark had taken on the role of producer, helping with any technical issues and getting the lighting adjusted. The girl from the front desk, Ava saw her nametag read *Kendra :),* had taken the phone off the hook while the interview was going on and had come over to sit with Ava, having sensed that she was nervous about how fast things were moving.

"This is exciting! Are you ready to be on TV?"

"I uh... I don't think I can."

"Sure you can! Look at how confident your dad is up there and he's a big nerd. You're the popular girl that's a badass priestess of the Unknown God with a legion of followers. You actually have more followers than any of the news stations on this interview have viewers." After Ava gave her a sideways glance, she clarified, "We don't have much to do most of the time up here. When Mark told me why you were coming I watched the video, you're awesome. You got this."

"Thanks. How long have you umm... worked here?"

"First season, I just finished school and am looking for a steady job in the area."

"Oh, congrats. What did you study?"

"Psychology and adolescent counseling."

"Ah. You're pretty good at it."

"Am I? Thanks."

"Let me bring Ava over," her dad said a bit louder and signaled for her. Kendra gave her a wink and she made her way over to sit by her dad. "Here she is, and I'm happy to announce together that we have found that the altar she discovered belongs to the Norse god Forseti. This is an exciting find, not only the first evidence that the old gods were brought to the Americas, but the first altar to Forseti we've ever found."

The various news people began asking questions as her father called on them.

"Dr. Tillmann, what makes you so sure this is an Altar to Forseti and not simply a sign for hunting or the well?"

"Great question, thank you. Generally speaking the Norse settlers would have erected signs with written language instead of symbols and placing it in a circle on the ground wouldn't be effective. Plus, it's out of the way and not visible on the path to the well. As for why we believe it to be Forseti we know there was an ancient story about Forseti assisting a group of Frisians set adrift on a rudderless ship, guiding them ashore and using the axe to draw a spring from the land. For that reason the axe and the oarless boat have been associated with Forseti, though there are very little contemporary accounts to corroborate this with. I'll be examining it further with my peers."

"Ava, how did you come upon this find?"

"Well," she began nervously, "we were here while my dad was authenticating a nearby well and I was wandering around making videos when I saw it beneath some leaves."

"And what made you think to make an offering and plea to it?"

"I don't know, I was just goofing for a video. I didn't think I'd ever really use it."

"Were you really being picked on by your brother? It appeared that you had been crying when you made it?"

"Yeah, a bit so I was angry at the time. I think we're about even now though." The reporters laughed as Ava glanced up at her brother, who seemed a bit... hurt?

"Dr. Tillmann, can you speculate on how the altar remained there, or was put there in the first place? We know that the settlement was founded by Leif Erikson and his people, who were Catholic and spread the religion aggressively where they went," a stodgy looking gentleman asked.

"It's tough to say right now. This is still a fresh discovery and I've been thinking about that. The best I can come up with is that most of the holumenn that crewed the vessel would have been lower class and not brought along by choice. It's reasonable that they still worshipped, or at least remembered, the old gods. When they found a fracture spring similar to the story of Forseti's spring in Frisia, they built an altar thanking him. They built it just out of site of the well and the approach so only those who went looking would see it, and they would have been fairly confident that Leif wasn't fetching his own water."

"Ava how does it feel to be a viral sensation?" a younger reporter asked.

"I'm still absorbing it. I only thought a few friends would see it at first."

"Was any of this staged? You recently posted another video of your brother being 'punished' and you found a mysterious altar. I have to ask how much of this is real," a man with grey hair asked. Ava noticed his nametag said CFTV.

"I umm... I just recorded what I was doing."

"Dr. Tillmann, is this a publicity stunt by the university to drum up buzz for this find?"

"No, absolutely not. Why would I use a child for that, let alone cheapen a valuable discovery?"

"So, you think your daughter's antics..." The man was cut off by her dad removing the reporter from the chat.

"Anyone else have questions?" her dad asked cheerily.

After a few more questions her dad brought Jake in and told everyone how good a sport he'd been through this and how much the kids really loved each other, just pick like any siblings. When the call was over the whole room sat and stared and tried to catch their breath.

8

Glitnir shined across the realm, its silver roof reflecting the sun brighter than it had in a millennium. Forseti walked to the viewing pedestal, feeling much stronger than he had since waking. He drew the blood to begin the ritual and focused on finding his priestess, his Ava.

This time, he immediately saw a large web covering the globe, showing lands that he was never able to see before with points of light indicating a worshipper. The brightest of the lights was coming from near where he had found Ava before.

Following the tethers indicating the connections between the followers, he soon found her in a building on the northern shores of a land he didn't know well. As his view neared, he was distracted by a strong pull near the building. Looking around he saw buildings that reminded him of Viking settlements and away from the shoreline the source of the energy. Moving quickly he soon found his altar, broken and long left in disrepair. He sensed a connection with the followers of old and soon noticed the spring nearby.

Did I make this? Could be my work. Why out here though, an hour's walk from the settlement? What's these bits near the altar stone? Colorful, small, perhaps some sort of currency? Let's get back to Ava, I need to figure out what's going on.

He found her quickly, now able to sense her easily. She was sitting with an older man, her father perhaps, and speaking to a glowing tablet. There were others around, including a boy child looking sullen.

"I am fairly confident that the altar is Forseti's," the older man said. "Very little is written about him in the scarce Norse texts we have, but the documentation of the spring in Fositesland and the Charlamagne era tale of the Frisian Lawspeakers, both support that what would become Forseti was associated with well springs. No other Scandinavian deities are associated with these symbols, especially combined. As I said, I'll need further discussion with my peers."

The glowing tablet spoke, though Forseti had trouble making out what was said. Moving his view to see the tablet he saw small faces moving and speaking. He was so absorbed with what he was seeing that he found himself startled when the man started speaking again, addressing the people on the tablet Forseti realized.

"It does seem coincidental that Ava found the altar to a judgement god and asked for help but it hasn't impacted my analysis. Really, if you look at the original video she asks for punishment and protection, which is a common thing to ask of a deity, and what we see could be perceived as judgement. Because we see judgement happen it's easy to think it was about judgement all along. It's like shooting a gun at a board and then drawing the target around the hole."

I like this guy. Wait, what did that tiny woman say?

"I think he likes candy," Ava said. "My first offering was Smarties chocolates like these." The girl proceeded to show one of the small colorful coins and immediately popped it into her mouth and started to chew. "A friend used nuts when she tried it and it backfired on her. I recommend chocolate for best results, but feel free to put your own spin on it!"

Chocolate? A food? Of course! She's making offerings of food, that's why I've regained strength so quickly. Her friends are making them too. Why is that girl over there talking into a small stone?

Going to the other girl in the room he saw another face on the device she was holding, they were talking back and forth.

"Hold on, I have another call coming in," she said. "Hello? Oh, hey, Trevor! Yeah, it's crazy. We never have anything exciting now we have news channels coming in to shoot pieces on the site and the village. I have to go, I have my mom on the other line..."

What is this power that lets them talk to one another through a viewing stone? Which realm are they talking to?

After observing for a while, and seeing the children exchange *numbers* with the other adults on their *phones*, Forseti began to understand the technology. The large tablet. *a laptop*, held much information that Forseti observed while watching over the man's shoulder. Forseti came to understand that nearly all information about him was gone, though it also appeared that information on all the Norse deities was limited.

"Ava, check it out," the boy that he now knew to be her brother said.

"You're being refreshed by a bunch of people. It's all over my front page."

Forseti looked at the phone in Jake's hand. He saw a young boy making an offering on a symbol of Forseti, what appeared to be a few small shiny pieces with paper sticking out the top. He was asking for judgement against his mother for burning his favorite meal.

Jake touched the phone and another image came through with what appeared to be bread on the symbol and speaking in a language Forseti didn't recognize, but could understand thanks to his godly gifts. This girl was asking for punishment against someone who had somehow run over her grandmother.

Forseti could feel a surge of energy and raised his view high above the world, looking at all the requests coming in and offerings made. His godly essence would settle most disputes, Midgardian issues rarely required his direct attention, but Forseti was a wise god, and had realized that popularity was crucial currency in the world he now found himself watching. Based on the videos of Ava's that he had now seen, people wanted to see results. He focused his mind and looked for opportunities for immediate satisfaction.

"Forseti, god of judgement! I beg of you to render a verdict on my wife for taking so long to choose a movie that we don't have time to watch it now," a man was saying over an offering of popcorn. *Seems a bit beneath me, but... okay.* While the man was still recording, Forseti focused on the glowing device in front of them, which seemed to be the source of his consternation with his spouse. A spark came from the back and a wisp of smoke began to rise.

"Forseti, hear me!" another commanded. "I ask for your judgement on these undersalted french fries." Forseti took a look around the brightly colored building they were in and determined the subject of the complaint was the small food the man had put out as an offering.

You're offering me the thing you're complaining about? Fine. A shout from the back drew the man's attention, and his camera. The fry cook had yelped and dropped his basket of fries back into the oil, as well as knocking the saltshaker in as waved his hand to remove the grease that had just burned him.

"Oh, Unknown God, in case you're not Forseti," another began, "cast your gaze upon my offering of the finest chocolate from Sweden and hear my plea. The man who destroyed my life still walks free. He took my money, my youth, my happiness. He found a new woman, and he sits there across the street in his new car while he drops off my children. Where's the justice?"

Forseti saw the offering laid out on a sheet of paper. It appeared to be a cut up sausage, though not the color of a sausage he'd ever seen. The man was visible outside in the horseless wagon he had seen at the other spots. The man was talking with the children and ordering them to hug the woman that accompanied them. They reluctantly did as they were told and ran to the house. The man turned to the woman and assured her they would like her more than their real mother before they knew it. As the vehicle began to move Forseti forced the car to turn, hitting a red post nearby. As a torrent of water sprayed up from the impact Forseti was caught off guard and was still staring when the mother came into the yard carrying her phone and recording the scene.

After a few more helpings of justice Forseti removed himself from the viewing surface and laughed to himself. As he walked back towards his throne he saw that his house was beginning to repair itself. The columns shone of gold, the floors a polished marble. His throne gleamed of silver atop the onyx dais. He walked to his private chambers, seeing his bed decorated with clean linens. A bowl of fresh water sat nearby and he pushed at it with his mind, seeing the water respond and make a small ripple. Grinning, he held out his hand and closed his eyes. With the sound of a wave crashing on a rocky shore he opened his eyes to see a golden axe held in his fist.

I am returned! The strength I feel flowing through me is amazing after days of weakness.

He walked his palace, taking inventory of the things that had not been repaired or replaced and found himself in front of the pedestal again. He faintly heard the voice of his priestess and took a closer look. He quickly found her at a building near the one they had been in earlier. She was in a bedroom now with her brother, her father appeared to be in a room nearby from which there was water running.

"You better be nice to me, I'm famous now *and* I have a god that can help me."

"I'm sorry, I never meant to be mean to you. I was just picking! I thought we were having fun."

"Uh huh, well, now you see how it feels."

"Just don't make anymore vids of me please, I don't want to be known as the guy getting beat up in your videos."

"No promises."

Jake turned away and focused on his phone, tapping it furiously. Ava pointed hers at her make-shift altar. Forseti could see it clearly now. A book of papers with his symbols and a heading that read Ava's Anti-Bully Altar! Her phone was plugged into a nearby wall with the cord lying across the book.

She had laid out some candies and began to speak. "Oh, Forseti, master of judgement. Now that my brother has been exposed for all to see, I ask that you once again show him your wrath for unfairly taking the bed instead of the pull-out couch."

Forseti looked at Jake, who appeared upset and rolled his eyes. "I'm, like, two feet taller than you."

"You shouldn't mess with a priestess of the old gods, especially one with the ability to livestream."

Forseti took a moment to evaluate the situation, seeing that Ava was still recording on her device. There were words flashing across as well as small symbols of hearts. There were people watching as it happened. He had to give the audience a message, one to cement his name.

The cord plugged into the wall sparked, causing the edge of the paper to begin to smolder. Ava shrieked and blew out the embers, Jake running to help her. Ava laid her phone down while she opened the window and her dad emerged from the other room, wet but clothed. After a few minutes he determined it to be the old wiring in the house they were staying in and tried to calm everyone down. Ava's phone was still lit with viewers watching and when she returned to pick it up she pointed it at the paper, showing the aftermath of her request. Some of the wording along the top had been burnt away and she focused on it a bit before talking to the viewers.

"Well, guys, that's all the excitement for one night."

Forseti studied his small priestess, and tightened his lips. He owed her his life and loyalty, but he also couldn't let his name be used as a weapon against the innocent. He glanced at the journal once more before retiring to his mansion.

Ava's A Bully !

9

"Good evening, My name is Riad Adam and this is RearView. Today, we have a special treat and a bit of levity. In northern Newfoundland it has been announced that an altar to a nearly forgotten Norse god has been found near the only Viking settlement in North America outside of Greenland. Interestingly, this was apparently only discovered because of a teenage girl filming Kuhlr videos while her archaeologist dad was investigating a nearby well. Let's take a look at the video that is going viral..."

Riad Adam, *RearView with Riad*, ICONnews

Forseti looked out from the doorway of Glitnir over the hills nearby. He could hear the clash of the Einherjar training in Valhalla, waiting for the day when they are called forth to battle the wolf Fenrir. He felt the winds coming from the hill where the Bifrost connects to the other realms and Heimdall stands vigilant. The enormous world tree, Yggdrasil, towered in the distance and Forseti watched for a while to see if the squirrel, Ratatosk, still scurried along the trunk carrying messages between the eagle and the wyrm. He remembered intercepting the message a couple of times while feeding the squirrel some nuts. They were always bitter and malicious, he snickered as remembered a particular line from the eagle—*Dear Nithhogg, had a gecko for brunch today. He was a more worthy competitor than yourself. Best regards.* Well, after a couple thousand years they were sure to be scraping bottom on their insults by now.

The mansions he could see, though still beautiful, were a faded memory of their grandeur. Where twisting vines and running harts once ruled was now low brush and overgrown fields. The cobbled street that his home sat on was worn smooth by the shuffling semi-awake inhabitants, but tangles grew along the edges and ruts had formed where stones had come loose. There was a chill in the air despite the shining sun that was warm on his face, the birds sang from their unseen nests.

Now, this is what I was yearning for. I feel fully rested and strong. I can push my will through to the other realms and I can judge once again.

He started at a leisurely pace down the road with no particular destination in mind. He saw Modi and Magni, Thor's sons, moving pieces of marble to repair a fountain and waved to them.

"Good day Uncle," Magni called. "You're looking healthy."

"I feel good, though I dare say I don't look quite as healthy as you two."

"Perks of being descendants of Thor," Modi added, "along with being given the most laborious jobs. I can't even remember what this fountain was for."

"If I recall correctly, it's a memorial of the harvest, therefore an honor to the Lady Sif."

"Then why are we doing this? Thrud is her daughter with our father." Magni complained.

"She is busy doing her duties as a Valkyrie. I've always thought of Sif as my mother too, so we will complete our task."

After a bit of small talk Forseti continued towards the ocean. The scent of apples caught his attention and he soon found the Giantess Gerda, wife of Frey. She seemed quite tired and worn out compared to Thor's sons, and Forseti realized it was due to her being not as well known in the modern world.

This strong and noble woman should be as known as any other. Her shimmering beauty inspired poets and artists, her presence causes the crops to grow, and she's an incredible hnefatafl player to boot!

He spent some time with her, eating apples and enjoying the sunshine while sitting in the tall grass. Rested, he continued his walk. As he approached the shore the smell of the salty water greeted him and he could hear the calls of the birds looking for their lunch. He sat on the rocks where the waves could just reach his feet and closed his eyes. It seemed odd to take such pleasure in rest and peace, considering his long slumber, but he decided it just wasn't the same if you weren't awake to enjoy the rest. The nine daughters of Aegir and Ran frolicked in the surf, and Forseti enjoyed listening to their muffled arguments. He spied a raven on a nearby rock that seemed to be scouring for crabs or insects. He knew the ravens reported all they saw to Odin, and he wasn't sure he wanted the Allfather to know his strength yet. Mimir had seemed to be hesitant to let the others know why Forseti was so quick to recover, so he decided that resting on the rocks a bit longer would be prudent and soon dozed off.

As the sun set, Forseti was awoken by a chill in the breeze. Ran stood nearby looking out at the sea, her daughters had left with the tide. In her hand she held her net, ready to snare unwary sailors.

"I don't see many sailors out here, darling."

"No, and there aren't many that drown in Midgard anymore either," she said with a watery voice. Ran had always been kind to him, despite her reputation as the evil and dangers of the deep sea. Forseti had judged a dispute between her and Freyja once. Sailors had encountered pirates and had died with their axes in hand, though their bodies were thrown overboard and sunk to the depths. Forseti had ruled that any who had killed an attacker in defense of the ship and retained their weapon would be given to Freyja, and the others would be Ran's. Both the goddesses agreed and left his court appeased.

"Are you well?" Forseti asked?

"I don't remember what it is to be well, I just know that I am." Ran answered, eyes focused on the horizon.

"Would you like me to help get you somewhere?"

"No, thank you though. This is where I am best served, waiting for my daughters to pull a soul under to feed upon."

Forseti said his farewell and began to walk back towards the halls of the gods. As he came upon Gladsheim he was greeted with music and light pouring from the building. The smell of freshly cooked meat was heavy in the air, as was the sound of clinking mugs. He entered the Hall of Odin and saw the assembled gods feasting and drinking like the days of old.

"Forseti!" a booming voice called out from the other side of the room. He saw Thor approaching, or at least he thought it was Thor, he appeared quite a bit thinner than he remembered. "I heard you were awake, but hadn't seen you about. Are you well?"

"I am, thank you. I'm regaining my strength slowly, but I think I'll be okay."

"Good to hear, brother. Every Aesir that wakes is cause to rejoice, we've been away too long."

"Are you well, Thor?" Forseti asked tentatively.

"I feel great! I might have more worshippers now than I did when my cults were still active."

"You just look, well, dehydrated."

"Oh, yes. That's the fashion on Earth now and how they choose to depict me."

"Earth?"

"That's what the humans call their realm these days. It's quite a bit different, I find it easier to call it Earth also, as it doesn't resemble the Midgard we knew."

"Thank you for explaining. I saw your sons earlier, they looked well and were being quite helpful."

"They're good boys. That reminds me, I need to find Sif and bring her the mead she sent me for. Good to see you, brother."

"You as well." Forseti grasped wrists with Thor and realized that even with his returned strength and Thor's apparent malnutrition, the thunder god was still far stronger than any other.

By the thrones he saw many members of the Council talking with other Aesir, Vanir, and Giants. Odin sat with his brothers, Villi and Vi, laughing merrily. His wife, Frigg, sat nearby talking with Idunn who was eating an apple.

"Greetings Forseti," Mimir said as he approached.

"Mimir, good evening. What's the occasion?"

"Being alive another day? Since when do we need a reason to feast?"

"I suppose you're right."

"You're nearly glowing, child, what have you gotten yourself into?"

"The humans," Forseti began, keeping his voice low and conspiratorial. "I don't understand how, but they're telling stories of me all over the realm. Lands I've never seen before are drawing altars to me and praying."

"Interesting. I too have felt the power coming from Midgard. It seems you've kicked up a lot of attention somehow."

"Earth."

"What?"

"Thor said it's called Earth now, not Midgard."

"If I wanted Thor's input I'd put on a pretty wig and ask for it."

Forseti continued into the throne area and greeted Odin and the other assembled gods. They cheered his return, raised mugs and haunches of meat in his honor, and they talked long into the night. Chants of *Skaal* danced in Forseti's mind as he passed out on his throne with the huntress Skadi asleep on his shoulder.

As the sun beat in through the open doorway, Forseti attempted to open his eyes. He determined it to not be worth the effort, however, and instead focused on getting his bearings through his other senses. He heard someone talking to the side near the head of the thrones. He couldn't determine what was being said, but could make out Odin's responses.

"Really? That many? How did that escape you? We had a deal that I recommend you hold to."

Hate to be whoever that is.

As footsteps went past him he opened his eyes in curiosity and could only make out dark hair and a green cloak before the shape disappeared through the doorway. Forseti adjusted Skadi's position a bit as his shoulder had gone numb and returned to slumber.

10

A small ship and axe symbol is shown on a table in front of a hamster.
The scene cuts to hands using precise tools to make a beautiful roast lamb
with cooked apples and green vegetables, in incredibly small scale.
The hands place the vegetables and apples in front of the hamster on a
small plate.
The lamb is presented on a small wooden plank and placed in the symbol.
Across the screen a plea is written as the scene fades
Requesting justice for animal abusers.
Kuhlr talk, user MicroNutrients, 227,000 likes

Ava continued to produce videos dedicated to Forseti, varying between
informational videos about the god with her father and occasional offerings
aimed at social justice causes. The general consensus after her live stream was
that it was a clever set-up aimed to take the harsh spotlight off of her brother
and people appreciated the gesture, continuing to add followers.

Her content tended to be more day-in-the-life silly videos similar to the
content she had been making before, but now widely shared and viewed. The
audios from her previous offering videos had continued to become heavily
reused, from her appeals to the Unknown god to her deciding to reevaluate her
decisions, she couldn't scroll her front page without hearing her own voice over
other videos. She certainly didn't mind, however. The attention was nice, and
the sponsorships / free stuff from companies looking for the next "viral" hit
were a great bonus.

The meme of Forseti dishing out judgement for minor infractions became
heavily entrenched with content creators escalating the intricacy of their
offerings, often for the simplest of misdeeds.

One popular video showed a bearded craftsman carving an intricate Celtic knot out of a bone in front of a fireplace. The screen panned to an axe symbol made of wrought iron in the fireplace, standing out above the burning wood.

The man spoke in a soothing, deep voice. "Forseti, bringer of justice, I humbly present this offering of a prized possession in exchange for punishment of one who caused offense against me."

The camera moved over the man's shoulder where a large golden retriever is seen staring hungrily at the bone the man had finished carving.

"Dodger, my prized hound, has betrayed me and eaten my slippers."

Torn up slippers came into focus behind the dog.

"May he be stricken with an itch he can't quite reach until his next bath." The man tosses the bone into the fire with the dog looking after it.

Jake had been friendly with Ava since their trip to the site, enjoying his own status beside her in their video interviews with various talk shows. He had even gotten interested in Norse and Germanic mythology, considering pursuing the subject as he began to apply to universities. Their father was overjoyed with his newfound attention and indulged him in all kinds of information and even allowed him to get a tattoo of Odin's ravens, Huginn and Muninn, on his bicep.

A small offshoot of videos from "victims" of judgement had sprung up with Jake as an unofficial figurehead. #JusticeForJake was trending on Kuhlr just behind #ForsetisJudgement and #ChipCanHands. The most popular of these were parodies of Ava's backfire video, from people making offerings on roofs they "fell" off of to sitting at a table and the chair breaking on them.

While most were tongue in cheek, Dr. and Mrs. Tillmann had noticed that a growing number were bitter or carrying a political message. They lacked understanding of the algorithms that social media uses so the more they watched this type, the more of it they saw and led them to believe that it was overtaking the app. In response, they limited Ava and Jake's exposure, though they were careful not to forbid the use of the app completely, mostly asking them to turn off direct messaging.

∽ ∽ ∽

Forseti found himself in high demand and struggling to keep up with requests. Through his glimpses into the world through his viewing mirror he had been able to put a lot of the technology and social aspects of his popularity into context, even if he didn't understand how the technology worked or what a request to "yeet" someone meant. He was continually amazed at how interconnected the world was and how fast travel had become.

Another request from a boy in a flying vessel complaining about his teacher giving him a lower grade for turning in his work late—didn't she realize he had been on a trip to Ebitha, wherever that was. A woman past her birthing years wishing judgement on her spouse for his dalliance with a younger maiden. A lot of requests to punish 'hackers' and cheaters on video games... he had learned about these games, which were capable of simulating battle using a similar technology as Ava's video sharing.

As his power and influence grew, more of his requests were able to be handled automatically, only involving himself personally when he wanted to conserve the energy the auto-handling took from him or for more complex and interesting requests.

"We were nearly done with our escape room, literally two puzzles from completing it," a red-haired woman said into the camera at an angle Forseti had come to know as the *breast angle*, sure it had her face in it, but with the overhead angle the bottom 2/3rds of the screen were cleavage. He may not be tech savvy, but he knew the videos that did the angle well got more applause, or *likes*, than others. "Just as I was getting ready to mix the ingredients for the potion, Mr. Mansplain over here jumped in with an 'Um, actually.'" The video shifted to a man with a hat and sunglasses shaking his head before returning to the practiced pose of the angle. "He tells me the recipe I chose was wrong, and it was really the recipe in the notebook from the drawer because the professor would have written it from his beloved recliner. So we make that mixture and the lights come on with the staff informing us we all died from poison inhalation. Forseti, I don't have a symbol handy, but please strike this fool down for not trusting his girl. I offer up the rest of this iced latte."

An offering of scraps? As the lady recorded, she stumbled on a crack in the sidewalk, causing her frozen coffee to splash into her chest before dropping it to the ground. Caught off guard by her gasp, the boyfriend in the background looks to her and doesn't see the dropped beverage. When he hurried forward to help her, he slipped on the ice and fell, pulling her down with him. The video ends with the couple seen laughing while trying to untangle themselves.

"Forset, as you were called by the Frisians, we ask for your judgement. We know you as Lawspeaker and that your word is final. We beg of you to settle the debate of the ages. Before us we've created a trolley problem," a young man with robes on said, showing a small railroad set with one engine facing a split in the rail. on one rail was a small doll, on the other was five smaller dolls. There appeared to be no doll in the train. "As is tradition, the train is set to run over the five victims, is it merciful to change the track to run over just the

48

one and save the five, minimizing the lives lost, but through action, causing the death of one, or is it ethical to allow the five to die through inaction?"

When the man finished his question the train began to move and close the gap. Forseti was unsure of how to proceed, he knew they were dolls, but his job was to judge! As the train came closer to killing five innocent dolls Forseti made his decision and moved the switch just a fraction of an inch, causing the train to derail and saving all the dolls.

"Well, that was unexpected. I suppose there's a lesson here, but I don't know what it is just yet."

"Hi, guys. Hank here," a man, apparently named Hank, said, "to talk to you about Forseti. Did you know he's really the Greek god Posei..." *Ugh, skip.*

"In our fanfic, we've been exploring Forseti's relationship with Hela," a bright-eyed girl said into the camera, "and the crisis it caused him, fearing he would have to judge *himself* if Loki found out."

Hela? I assume she means Hel. She is beautiful, well... on one side. I wouldn't be too worried about Loki, though; he bred with a horse. I suppose Hel is quite a bit better than any of his other kids. Where has Loki been? I've heard him mentioned in many videos so I'm sure he's awake.

"These cuck liberals think tripping on a shoelace is punishment from some heathen god. What a bunch of idiots. Wear slip-on shoes like the babies you are, and quit posting your blasphemy in the open," a skinny man with glasses and a bow tie was saying. Forseti moved to the next image, he had found that anyone using that tone hadn't been worth his time.

"I'm Megan, this is Morgan," a bubbly girl with dark hair and heavy eyeshadow said. Megan was wearing a black shirt and was not skilled in *the angle.* Morgan, a taller girl standing beside her, had light red hair and green eyes, her eyeshadow was not as heavy, but gave the impression of wings. "Unlike all these other basic bitches offering up their pumpkin spice wheat grass shots or whatever, we're offering something one of The Old Gods might actually want. We got this bag of chicken heads from a local butcher."

The camera showed a brown bag in a blue cooler. The cooler was on a tree stump with the oarless boat and double-sided axe inked onto it. Morgan moved the cooler to the center.

"With this offering, we request retribution on the guy that tried to force himself on Morgan at the college party last weekend. He was so gross and tried to get her to go upstairs with him, luckily we're only 19, so Morgan was only drinking seltzer drinks and knew to leave."

The camera recentered on the bag that allegedly contained bird heads. A match went into the cooler and the bag was soon burning.

Why would I want chicken heads? That's the least tasty part of the chicken! A lad tried to force himself on this young woman in a dishonorable manner? I can not abide that, I rule that during his most vigorous years no child will be born to him. Not until he has settled with one woman in his older years shall he know fatherhood. His bloodline shall suffer for his cowardice.

From his view high above the realm, Forseti could see the altars that had been made in his name. The area known as The Americas was practically covered in spots of light, with other spots spreading around from there into parts of the world previously unknown to him. He felt strong, possibly as strong as he had ever been in the years before the decline of the gods. Leaving the looking glass he took in his home, now glowing brightly across Asgard, visible from all around.

11

"As if social justice warriors weren't already enough of a threat to free speech, now they're making offerings to pagan gods right out in the open and cheering each other on! Earlier this week one of these so-called *Crusaders* made a video asking for me to be physically harmed in response to our reporting on the border crisis..."
Daisy Dunn, *The Final Word,* Freedom First News Network

The waves caused the ship to rise and fall rhythmically before breaking on the shore. Forseti relaxed on the deck with Balder, drinking ale and laughing about old memories. He had gotten used to the mental discomfort of his old memories overlapping the new reality that all the other gods seemed to recall. He had spent a lot of time on Hringhorni lately, enjoying the company of his friend / father. As Forseti's own legend grew, he noticed Balder gaining strength as well by his association. They hoped that Nanna, Balder's wife, would rise soon, but so far had not seen her.

"I haven't had a flyting like that since Odin disguised himself and challenged Thor and I in the feasting hall. He defeated the both of us and much mead was drunk that night." Balder was reminiscing. Flyting was a hobby of the wise gods and involved insulting each other to poetic verse and the winner was determined by the crowd's reaction. Balder had been a gifted flyter and his bouts with Loki had been the subject of retellings and wood carvings in their time.

Loki again. Why does he keep coming up, yet I haven't seen him?

"Father?" Forseti interrupted. "Where is Loki? I've heard he is awake, but I haven't seen him in any halls."

"He comes from time to time, but he is largely isolated to working in the other realms for Odin."

"Working for Odin? That's odd. Loki rarely did anything without being forced. What kind of work?"

"Gathering information from what I understand. As a shapeshifter he's always been able to travel Midgard easily. He reports on what's happening there and influences their people to remember us and restore us to power."

"I see," Forseti said. "Are we sure the Giant is to be trusted? He's caused much mischief, as well as killing you and blocking your return from Hel."

"Yes, he is quite the prankster. Odin assured us that he has him under control, that he holds power over him. I don't trust Loki, but I trust in the Allfather

"Has Sigyn returned?"

"Who?"

"Sigyn, his wife."

"Oh, yes, of course. No, I don't believe she has."

By now he was used to seeing the look of an Aesir suddenly remembering things long forgotten and not from their current reality. Sigyn wasn't a part of the narrative on Earth. If Loki was influencing events, why hadn't his wife been a part of the stories? Why hadn't Forseti? The boat continued to rock gently and Balder seemed content to rest. He bid him farewell and began to walk back to his own hall. He wanted to give the matter more thought and didn't wish to cause discomfort to his father if his thoughts didn't match the knowledge he currently had.

He stood over the mirrored glass and offered the blood required to see the world. Pushing aside the indicators of those asking for judgements and looking through the interconnected web of his followers he looked for information on Loki.

He wasn't able to find the trickster himself but could see his influence. The web of worshippers and celebrants of Loki was even heavier than Forseti's, causing him to wonder at what Loki had accomplished. He focused on the individual dots but couldn't find any actively celebrating or discussing Loki aside from seeing an occasional writing of his name on a wall or book. Realizing that he wasn't going to get anywhere that way he retreated from the glass and went to his throne to try remembering his interactions with the Giant.

The binding of Fenrir, that was the first I spent any time with Loki. He knew something was going on. The morning had been cool and a light wind blew over lake Amsvartnir. The Aesir had summoned the great wolf to the island of Lyngvi to continue their game with him. The beast arrived along with his father, Loki. As their boat slid over the inky black water, Fenrir approached the bow and leaped to the shore.

"What do you have this time?" He asked, his voice guttural and booming.

"A different approach," Tyr responded. "You've bested our strongest chains and fetters so we wished to try our strongest cloth."

"So many witnesses to this challenge." Fenrir looked around and let his gaze linger on the assembled gods. Odin, Tyr, Frey, and Thor stood at the front along with Forseti, with other Aesir attending behind them.

"Word of your great strength has spread. When you broke the great chain Dromi, pieces flew so far as to take your legend along anywhere they landed."

Loki stepped ashore as the boat stopped. "A cloth you say? What challenge is a bit of fabric?"

"See for yourself," replied Frey.

Loki took the cloth and tried to break it, unable to after much effort. The Aesir took it and tried to rip it as well, unable to even when Thor and Odin pulled against each other.

"I don't believe my fame will grow by tearing a bit of cloth. If it was made with trickery, however, I don't want it on my legs," Fenrir growled.

"There is no trickery here. If you are truly the wolf of prophecy you'll be able to break such a thin band. If not, you will have proven that you are nothing for us to fear and we will release you," Odin teased.

"I know a thing or two about tricks, Fenrir, I don't like this," Loki said, not taking his eyes off the band.

"If I am unable to break free I feel that it would be a long time until you released me. Instead of questioning my courage, I will accept if one of you will place your hand in my mouth as a show of good faith."

None of the gods moved, and Forseti could have sworn Odin leaned backwards just a hair. A second later, Tyr lifted his right arm and let Fenrir take his hand in his mouth. The gods bound Fenrir's legs with the ribbon, anchoring it to a massive boulder.

Fenrir strained against his bindings, but was unable to snap a single thread, the mythical materials made of impossible ingredients held. The gods cheered and smiled at each other, except Tyr. Forseti was watching Tyr as he closed his eyes, knowing what was coming. Fenrir closed his mouth, taking Tyr's hand.

He lashed out again, but Tyr had backpedaled as soon as his arm was free. Fenrir lashed out, attempting to bite anyone foolish enough to get near. Thor strolled forwards with a sword, wedging it into Fenrir's giant mouth. With the hilt on his bottom jaw and the point pressuring the roof of his mouth Fenrir

53

was unable to bite, he howled in rage and sadness.

"What are you doing?" Loki cried out. He tried to help his son, but the other gods held him back as the wolf was anchored to yet another, stronger, boulder. "You can't just leave him here, why not just kill him? Forseti, you are said to be wise in judgement—I demand judgement for this deception!"

Forseti looked back to Loki and nodded. He walked away from Fenrir and signaled all to follow. On the other side of the island the cries of the wolf were still heard, but able to be spoken over. Loki laid out his argument that the Aesir must be punished for giving false information as well as the cruelty of the punishment they had bestowed on Fenrir, despite him not having committed any crime other than being born. Forseti considered the argument and responded. "I agree with Loki that the Aesir must not be allowed to spread false information and need be punished. As it happens, Tyr has already paid the price agreed upon by the parties. Fenrir outlined that if it were a trick, his payment would be the hand of a god—which he received. Fenrir has been bound because of the prophesy of him devouring the Allfather. The gods can't kill Fenrir and defile their lands, knowing that he is innocent so far."

"Can't we at least take the sword out?" Loki was pleased.

"No Aesir would put their hand near the Sun eater and you are unable to remove it. You are welcome to try, but I fear you would only cause more harm." Forseti's memory faded away as he watched Loki examining the sword for a way to release it while the drool from the wolf began to form a river below them.

He was quite upset, understandably. My judgement was fair, though Loki remained cold to me from there. He did go on to be involved in the death of Balder, those are the last interactions I remember with him.

෴ ෴ ෴

All the nine realms felt the death of Balder. While some of the Aesir rode off to Hel to beg the release of his soul or birthed children to enact vengeance on the perpetrators, Forseti had been tasked with judgement. Vengeance was temporary, pleading with the goddess of death was a hope, Forseti's judgements were final. The narrative had been established, and the stories told throughout Asgard.

Balder had dreamed that his end was coming, Odin traveled to Hel and saw they were preparing a feast for his arrival, Frigg went and got every living and non-living thing in the cosmos to promise to cause no harm to the much beloved god. She recalled to a disguised Loki that she had not gotten a promise from the mistletoe for it was so small and weak. Loki had created a spear of mistletoe and approached Hoth, the blind god, who sat to the side while the others threw objects at Balder, celebrating his immortality.

Loki aimed Hoth's hand to help him honor Balder, having given him the mistletoe spear. Balder fell immediately to the projectile, Hoth had been killed and Loki bound. Forseti's job was to determine the truth of the story and deem the punishment sufficient.

He went to visit Loki in his cave, along with Skadi, where he had been caught by the other gods and was now imprisoned. Loki admitted to his role in creating the spear and aiming Hoth's hand.

"That does kind of make your defense tougher." Forseti informed the trickster.

"Yeah, not sure the punishment fits the crime here, though." Loki grunted.

"You killed Odin's son, he killed yours and imprisoned you."

"He turned one of my sons into a wolf and made him attack his brother, spreading his entrails through the cave which the gods turns to steel and bound me with."

"In all your dealings with Odin, it didn't occur to you that killing his son would result in an... *outsized* retribution?"

"Well, I didn't intend to get caught."

"The death of Balder has long been known to be the first sign of Ragnarok. Why bring that about?"

"Ragnarok is inevitable. All will fall and be reborn, why fight prophesy?"

"Why hurry it along?" Forseti asked with some exasperation.

"The answer of one who kneels to another."

"Why disguise yourself and prevent the release of Balder from Hel?"

"I couldn't allow my daughter to lose her guest of honor so easily, could I?" Loki deadpanned. Forseti considered that a confirmation of the rumor. Sigyn, Loki's ever-faithful wife, sat nearby. She had come after Loki had been caught to stay with him. Forseti noticed her sneer a bit when Loki called Hel his daughter. Hel, along with Fenrir and the world-serpent Jormungandr, had been children of the Giantess Angrboda.

"Your punishment here is just, you killed the most beloved of the Aesir and in return lost a child and were imprisoned to keep you from further meddling."

Loki and Sigyn looked away from him then, her to hide her tears and him to hide his rage.

"However," Forseti continued, "the punishment does not address you disguising yourself and stopping the efforts to return Balder. For continuing to rob the nine realms of his presence, I've brought Skadi along to add to your punishment as well as fulfill a promise she made to you long ago. For as long as Balder remains in Hel, this snake she hangs now will drop its venom on to you. Sigyn, while innocent of any crime, you've been a part of his antics for too long. You may stay here with this bowl and catch the venom from the serpent. You are not obligated to, however."

Loki lashed out in rage then. "You'll pay for this, rassragr! You're a coward!"

At that Forseti and Skadi left the cave. Hours later Sigyn went to empty the bowl and venom dripped onto Loki's face. His thrashing at the burning caused earthquakes on Midgard.

12

A small raven appears on screen with subtitles.

"Hi, I'm Forseti the Raven! I'm ready to render judgement," the text reads. The camera view changes to an overhead shot of a white mat with the double sided axe symbol. There are 2 bins set up beside each other with a treat dispenser attached. The bins are labeled as Cohen and Johnson, the two leading Democratic candidates in the primaries.

"Today we're choosing which candidate is worthy of victory."

The raven proceeds to pick up small baubles and place them in bins, each drop dispensing a small treat. At the end of the video more items had been placed in the box labeled Cohen.

"Cohen is judged worthy by Forseti. Tune in tomorrow for our look ahead to the Kentucky Derby!"

Kuhlr talk, user JinxTheRaven, 362,000 views

Loki was set free, though. Odin is using him on Earth. Something doesn't feel right. Forseti rose from his throne and headed to Odin's hall to ask about Loki's activities. He passed halls to other gods still not awake or at strength, decrepit compared to his own fully rebuilt palace. He reflected on those gods, remembering what he could and yearning for their realm to be whole again. He entered Gladsheim and approached the Allfather.

"Odin, may I ask for your wisdom?" he said, bowing his head momentarily.

"Of course, what troubles you, Forseti?"

"My thoughts lately have been of Loki and his crimes. I have been told he is free and in your service now. Do you know if has been changing our stories as he influences the Midgardians?"

"What are you insinuating, child?" Odin asked dryly. "Do you believe I'm not in control of him?"

"No, Allfather. It's just that..."

"Or is it that you believe I've told him to change our story?"

"No! Of course not..."

"Loki reports his activities to me and gives insight into how our efforts are being received. His work has returned many, though some aren't as attractive to modern Midgardians and his efforts lead nowhere. My poor Balder has barely been recognized in more than a title of some... *game*. You asked for wisdom, but only pester me with assertions. What is it you seek?"

"Did Loki erase me? I've seen the stories of old and how they're told now. Stories I was in, but no mention of me. There's altars and monuments all over the Viking lands yet not one of mine still stands."

"I can not spend time on your squabbles with Loki. If he left you out of stories as he told them, then you would need to speak to him as to why. Any indication he is working against our best interests and he is returned to the cave."

"What power do you hold over him?"

"His freedom, that is all."

Forseti turned to leave and experienced a flashback. He was sitting here, in the hall with many of the other Aesir. Odin stood before many of those assembled and reported on his activities. He had freed Loki and put him to work on Midgard. Belief was dwindling and he believed keeping the trickster on a short leash would allow him to influence the writers of the time. He remembered feeling weak, the others too. They all agreed to the plan, putting their faith in Odin.

Forseti left the hall and walked up the hill to the Bifrost. The bridge connected Asgard to the other realms and would be the path that Loki would need to take. The imposing Heimdall stood watch, ever vigilant for attack.

"Heimdall, old friend."

"Forseti! It is good to see you again. How long have you been back? I don't get much news here anymore, not too many traveling between the realms."

"Not long, a couple of weeks. I'm sorry I haven't visited sooner, I will be sure to come more often. I don't believe you need anyone to tell you news, however, Far-Seer."

"This is true," Heimdall chuckled.

"Can you tell me," Forseti ventured, "has Loki crossed recently, and has he been up to anything detrimental to us?"

Heimdall's face soured at the name of his old nemesis, the one foretold to kill him at Ragnarok. "He comes through occasionally, doing his work for Odin. I don't understand much of what he does in Midgard, mostly it seems he inserts himself into dreams or makes people think of certain things."

"Have you seen anything else? Anything that would prove he's been harming us?"

"Nothing of note. He's been doing his work for a thousand years though, both before and after I fell asleep."

"You slept as well?" Forseti asked.

"Of course, we all did. Loki ensured there were writings and stories to be told that would reawaken us, but Odin assured us it was inevitable we would be forgotten for a time. The Christians were too powerful then."

"Do we know for sure that Loki slept? Is it possible he was left alone for a time?"

"It's possible, things got a bit hazy there for a while. If he had been up to anything nefarious I would have found it. After all, you're never really alone when I'm watching." Heimdall said with a wink.

"What's that supposed to mean?"

"Remember that time when you stole Fulla away from her duties to Frigg? The virgin maiden to Odin's consort..."

"You didn't! You haven't told anyone, have you?"

"No." Heimdall laughed. "I've seen more than my share of Aesir, Vanir, Midgardians, and Giants getting up to things they'd rather keep secret from others. You've nothing to worry about Forseti."

"I'd nearly forgotten Fulla. Has she returned?"

"I don't believe so."

Forseti thanked Heimdall and took in the view of the burning rainbow bridge. He felt another flashback come on and soon saw Loki walking across towards Midgard. He hadn't trusted Odin's plan to release Loki and walked him to the bridge to ensure nothing happened while still inside Asgard. Loki had glanced back and smirked before disappearing into the distance.

Back in his mansion he paced the floor. *There's more to this than I'm seeing. Why am I fixated on this troublemaker? I feel as if there's something just out of reach.* His mind raced as he stared at his blank viewing mirror. He felt his mind flickering, reaching for a memory. He embraced the feeling and let his mind wander, soon he saw himself standing over the mirror, observing Midgard. He saw Loki telling stories to scholars and poets and working to preserve pieces of art depicting the gods. As he went to turn away he heard a crash, he saw Loki destroying vases with Forseti's story. As he watched he saw his own altars being destroyed or claimed by other religions, some pointed towards the sites by Loki in disguise. The mirror showed Loki's face, dirty and filled with rage, as he set fire to libraries of Germanic and Norse writings. Soon Forseti saw himself collapse in the flashback, this is where he had fallen asleep, after watching Loki destroy his legacy and being unable to intervene.

⌐ ⌐ ⌐

"So, our chicken heads video did really well," Megan started, "even though it did get a lot of angry comments from vegan Kuhlr."

"It wasn't even real chicken heads," Morgan replied while rolling her eyes, "if they had paid attention they would have been able to see the melting ping pong balls as the bag opened."

"I think it's safe to say they weren't looking that hard at what we told them were bird parts."

"That's not our fault. Also, who cares? We got like forty-five thousand views on that vid. Gotta break a few cups if you want to be the center of the Kuhlr talk... or something like that."

"Yeah, we need to follow up though. Those are good numbers, but this chick made a stone altar that was actually a cake and it's at like 150k."

"She's not wearing a bra, Meg, I don't think anyone cares about the cake. Well, maybe not that cake because she turned around and *dayum.*"

"Focus your bi-brain here, we need numbers woman!"

Megan had been captivated by the story of little Ava from Canada and her rise to internet celebrity. She insisted that if that girl could do it from "Literally the dandruff laden scalp of the world", then two cute goth girls from Indiana could do it. Morgan agreed and went along with her. Meg had been her best friend since junior high when she intervened on Morgan's behalf against a teacher that was teasing her about her chunky soled boots. Morgan was new to the school and had been intensely anxious about her appearance, she had matured early and liked to wear baggy clothes and taller shoes to look more proportional. She had gotten quite tall since and adapted a more prurient wardrobe, but she always loved the pimply girl that accused a teacher of being a weird pervert to draw the attention away from her.

Megan had been drawn to Morgan since she first saw her. She stood out among the brightly clothed students and embodied a drab muse. She had moved from Indianapolis to their backwater town and Megan hadn't met anyone else in their town she would describe as "not a Friday night football fanatic dork." She had been working up the courage to approach her and ask to hang out when she saw her being questioned by her creepy math teacher. There was a rumor he made pretty girls sit up front so he could see under their skirts. Morgan looked upset and Meg couldn't help herself. "Why are you harassing her? Why are you such a weird pervert? Come on Morgan!" That had been that, they were inseparable from that moment. Morgan helped Megan become more comfortable expressing herself, mostly in black, and Megan helped Morgan learn the ins and outs of their town and which weirdos to avoid.

"I'm betting skinny pale goth in a black bikini making an offering would do well," Meg teased.

Morgan was pretty sure Meg was not into girls, but she had made jokes about her doing bikini vids enough that she was starting to question herself. Had she misread their friendship? Was she missing out on perks? *Let's push back a bit and find out.* "Probably not as well as Big Titty Goth Girlfriend, you're a whole trending category on some sites."

"Sites you're visiting?"

"Maybe."

Meg laughed and trailed off talking about them doing a vid together on the beach in a very business-like manner while resuming her phone scrolling. *Well, that doesn't tell me anything.*

They continued their strategy session, deciding to play on their already mildly successful creep factor so as not to isolate their burgeoning following of what they assumed were either horror fans or chicken haters. It needed to be their best production yet, after all—Ava really hit the big time when her follow up trashcan video posted. With the right *My Chemical Romance* track and effects there was sure to be a Hot Topic sponsorship around the corner. Morgan was planning to go to school for film and Megan had always loved doing makeup and special effects, it was time to make their portfolio piece. First, though, Morgan had to call off sick to her job at Panera Bread.

"I don't know, like, my lip has a sore and I'm having really bad cramps. I don't know if I'm getting my period or having a herpes flare up, but I can't be in front of the public today." She hung up the phone and looked at Megan, who was giving her a raised eyebrow. "That was my shift lead Gary, he gets uncomfortable about anything girly and doesn't push the issue, plus I don't want him thinking I'm a viable mate."

They went to their rooms and changed into their most "endorsable" outfits, grabbed their gear and headed out. They jumped into Megan's aging Ford hatchback and started driving to Ouabache State Park. Morgan watched the trees as they passed and clouds turning red with the setting sun. She had forgotten to eat dinner, assuming she would eat at work. Meg wouldn't stop to get drive-through, as she wanted to be sure they got the right lighting and, "I have the blood packs cooled, if they get too warm it'll be runny." *There had better be food afterwards or my blood covered face won't be the scariest thing she sees.*

After finding a parking spot at the far end of the lot away from the families packing up from pool and picnics they unloaded their makeup bags and small battery powered ring light. They followed a walking trail until they found a nice break in the canopy and turned off the path. After some debate they settled on a fallen tree that was mostly in shadow. Morgan set the lighting to make sure they wouldn't be bleached out by the light falling in the area behind them while Megan worked on drawing up a mark of Forseti. She used some of the fake blood as well as some slimier bits of foliage from along the stream nearby. They applied their stage makeup and began their intro, they needed to get it right and get the gore shots before the sun moved much lower.

13

The railing of a bridge shows in the foreground with a river not far below. A hand is seen tossing a rope with a large magnetic disk attached over the edge. White writing pops onto the screen, each line fading as the next appears.

I've been magnet fishing for 2 years
I've found some pretty cool stuff
But mostly, it's trash that should have been recycled
Can Forseti punish people that litter the waterways?

The magnet is pulled back up with a small hatchet attached, the boat symbol is carved into the blade.

Kuhlr talk, user MagFisherMatt, 85,000 views

Forseti stormed from his hall and began walking without a destination. He wanted to seek out Mimir for advice, but knew he would be with Odin, who Forseti wasn't prepared to face in his current state.

He did it intentionally! I knew something seemed off, but why? To what end? Simple vindictiveness for the snake thing? That seems unlikely. What did he offer Odin to convince him to release him, and was this part of the plan? How many others were caught up in his deeds and their memories destroyed?

As his mind raced, he continued walking ever downhill. A raven followed lazily behind, occasionally getting sidetracked by a meal, but never losing him. The light was fading, yet Forseti continued to walk.

He'll pay for this. I may have lost time, but my following is growing, I'm getting stronger. I'll investigate this further now that I know what I'm looking for and take my findings to Odin, when he finds he was tricked as well Loki will be punished more than ever before.

Forseti soon found himself at the base of Yggdrasil, the world tree. There was no serpent, squirrel, or eagle in sight, all was calm around the massive tree. He found a suitable root and sat to continue his inner raging. Soon a wild horse came near the tree and stood gazing at Forseti.

"What do you want? I'm in a foul mood and have no apples for you."

"I'm not a big fan of apples if we're being honest." The horse replied in a nasally voice that Forseti placed immediately.

"Loki!" Forseti shot out of his seat and closed on the horse, but before he was able to reach him Loki had transformed into a large Crow and flew into a high branch.

"Relax, Forseti. I've come to talk. I've heard you've been asking around about me."

"I've been looking for who I should strangle for attempting to erase me!" Forseti shouted as he looked around for a stone to get the bird with.

"Well, I'm afraid you're literally barking up the wrong tree."

"I'm not barking! What do you take me for? I saw you destroying my record before I went to sleep, you made sure no one would remember me."

"Those things are true, the goal was to eliminate the memories of you, weaken your position in the council and eventually remove you completely. The fact still stands though that *I* did not decide on that fate."

"Don't toy with me trickster. You work for Odin, are you saying the Allfather ordered you to destroy my artifacts and belongings?"

"Well, I'd never put words in your grandfather's mouth, but I think you need to think a bit harder. Sure, I wouldn't mind some revenge, but why go through all that effort? I wouldn't stand to gain anything other than satisfaction and that isn't worth the time for me. You think I did this? Fine, but watch your back. I'd hate for you to focus too hard on the enemy in front of you and miss the one behind you."

Forseti looked behind him and saw nothing but a small bit of chain on the root he had been sitting on. He picked it up and examined it, chain links looking as if they had been forged from an animal's arteries and intestines. *Loki's chain from the cave. What did he mean by that? Is he saying that the other gods were involved?*

"We're back!" Megan started with a close up on herself. "Forseti was so pleased with our blood offering that he requested we send more, speaking to us in our restless sleep. To truly unlock the power of the old gods, blood must be spilled for him and him only."

A muffled squeal is heard in the background as she pans the camera to the mark.

"Today we will honor him as he commanded and welcome his judgement. This mark borne of blood and viscera will serve as our altar. The sacrifice? My most precious possession." She looked sad as she panned the camera once more to show Morgan, gagged with a T-shirt and wide eyed with panic.

Her Ramones t-shirt was carefully torn and dirtied to show a struggle, but also reveal the hint of a leather top below. *Branding.* She squealed through the cloth again and mumbled something incoherent. Megan picked her up roughly, showing that her hands were tied behind her back and her ankles were bound as well. She laid her across the fallen tree, her neck exposed above the symbol on the ground below. She held her in place as she moved to grab the knife nearby and showed the knife above Morgan's panicked face before stopping the camera.

"And, cut!"

"Reagh?" Morgan asked through the cloth. Her hands and gag were authentic, no better way to get the effect.

"We can't break continuity, keep the gag in so it looks the same and I'll grab the blood packs. We'll do the first-person stab shot first and then finish with the blood leaking into the symbol."

They had rehearsed the scene a few times when prepping at home. Both had worked the stage crew for their high school's drama department and were familiar with angles and effects. The camera would be positioned along the knife handle as it approached Morgan. The dark area beside her neck along with her hair as she moved her head the other way would cover the motion, also allowing Megan to squirt blood with her camera hand from above the phone and have fresh blood as she pulled the camera away. Megan would make two stabs and let the camera linger for a second on the motionless and blood splattered Morgan, then move on to the closing shot.

Megan laughed as they positioned the blood bag for the "money shot" on Morgan's neck. Morgan rolled her eyes and grunted through the shirt. They did the first stab, showing the metal of the blade. As the stab landed Megan squirted the blood from the small valve in the bag, it hit the side of her neck perfectly and she had gotten some down the blade as well. She pulled away; the shot looked great. Morgan was twitching just a bit as Megan stopped the camera.

"Okay, I'll grab the prop knife and throw blood on it now so we can do the *real* stab." The plan was to intercut the fake knife covered in blood either when the screen darkens in a shadow or worst case from the upstroke of the first stab.

With the blood on the blade, it didn't need to look as realistic and solid, it would be harder to tell the blade was retractable for the stab that shows hitting the skin. Megan stood up from her kneeling position resting her knife hand on the tree. Blood squirted from the pressure on the bag and she jumped back a bit, stumbling on the ring light set up behind them.

Her phone began to slip from her now slick hand, and she reached for it out of reflex to save a falling phone. Years later, she would recount that her mind entered slow motion at this point, remembering every detail even if her body couldn't respond fast enough.

She opened her phone hand just enough for the knife to start slipping, her reflexes hadn't accounted for a fairly heavy kitchen knife and bag of corn syrup. She saw her other hand closing in to cradle the phone. She could see Morgan's right eye through the gap between her fingers, widening with the realization that the knife had started to move.

Morgan began moving her head to the side oh so slowly. Megan's left hand finally arrived to clasp the phone, but the collision only knocked the knife the rest of the way out of her control. Megan released the phone and shot after the blade, noticing that she had hit the record button again in the fumble.

The phone video would go on to be analyzed by many professionals in many professions. In the opening frames Morgan's face can be seen panicking and moving to the side. She's already bleeding from the side of her neck.

As the camera rotates Megan's hand can be seen alongside the knife handle moving quickly, she appears to be putting her full weight behind the thrust. The camera falls below Morgan's hair and while it's bouncing a scream is audible. It's generally agreed to be two screams, one muffled and one scared.

The phone comes to rest on a twig, barely showing the forest floor and the edges of the symbol shown earlier. Megan's shoes are seen running away from the tree as screams echo through the area. A thick liquid begins to run into the symbol.

Devilry in Decatur flashes across the screen

"Our top story tonight, a teenage girl has been murdered in a state park in Indiana. Sources from inside the investigation that declined to be identified say it appears that the girl was bound, gagged, and sacrificed by her roommate to the pagan god Forseti, who has recently been popular on social media..."

Doug Hatcher, *The Hatchet,* Freedom First News Network

Megan ran back to her car to call the police. She was covered in blood and dirt, her clothes ripped from her falls on the pathway as the sun was no longer piercing the tree canopy. When she reached her car and was able to get a signal she realized that she needed to clean the blood from her hands to unlock the phone. She began wiping her hands in the nearby grass and promptly vomited. Stopping for the first time brought reality to her as the adrenaline faded. She kneeled on the grass and cried. *What are you doing?! Time is wasting, she needs you!*

"911, what's your emergency?"

"I need an ambulance at Oubache State Park, main parking lot!" Megan said quickly, focusing on the task at hand.

"While I work on dispatching a unit can you tell me the nature of the problem?"

"I..." Megan opened and closed her mouth a few times, unable to bring herself to say the words.

"Ma'am?"

"I think... I think I killed my best friend." The wall Megan had tried to build to get through the call collapsed as Megan fell to the ground, dropping her phone.

"Ma'am? Did you say you killed your friend? Ma'am?" The dispatcher never heard Megan's voice again aside from gasps and heavy sobs. She dispatched police to the site with an advisement that the caller may be armed and unstable. She stayed on the line listening to Megan until police arrived and hung up the call. She dried her own tears that had been shed in sympathy for the possible killer on the other end of the call.

Morgan was pronounced dead on arrival. The knife had severed her carotid artery. The crime scene photos showed a pale girl in black clothes lying backwards over a fallen tree. Her body was mostly clean, her head had been hanging towards the ground, keeping the blood spray away from her clothes. The macabre symbol below her head was filled with blood, thick and dark as oil in the night sky. The knife was found nearby, apparently Megan had pulled it out and then dropped it before retrieving her phone and running. The prop knife was laid nearby along with the stage blood bags.

Megan was taken to the police station and questioned. She told them everything, gave them her unlocked cell phone, and was held for a psychological evaluation and pending charges from the district attorney. Officers and investigators would report that she was cooperative and forthcoming with information. She was formally arrested for involuntary manslaughter the next day.

The media reaction to the event was immediate.

"Can you believe," began FFNN host Daisy Dunn, "these mainstream social media sites, which we already know to suppress conservative family and religious views, have allowed this demon worshiping to get to the point where impressionable youth see murder and violence as entertainment?" Daisy's sculpted blonde hair barely moved as her fingers pointed angrily at the camera and her lips pursed. "Tonight, we'll speak with Family Today's founder, Nicole Byrne, on how to talk to your children about false idols before it's too late."

Religious groups put out press releases asserting that the problem could be tracked back to not allowing prayer in schools and encouraging parents to bring their children to church regularly to gain clarity. Further, nearly every release would go on to say, if you are unable to make an offering at church, a donation through the church's website would ensure that they were able to continue their outreach programs to teenagers afflicted with this addiction to social media and technology.

Politicians, deep in their run up to the presidential elections, used the tragedy to appeal to their bases. Incumbent President, Todd Ridgway, echoed the conservative media's talking points while ensuring that the socialist media would be held responsible for their roles in warping the minds of America's children. Democratic nominee, Thomas Cohen, took the stance that mental health care for children needed to be universally available and while encouraging creativity, that safe places to create were essential, such as after school programs.

Middle aged talk show hosts talked at length with psychologists and parent activists about technology addiction, clout chasing, the breakdown of the family unit, and celebrity reactions to the news. Serious conversations were held over coffee mugs full of water with well dressed people discussing human sacrifice and trying to get in the head of the girls now at the center of the news.

One psychologist, renowned for a book they wrote 30 years earlier on the influence of violent cartoons, had this to say. "I've long warned of the effects of the media on children, whether it was animated rabbits with bombs or video games that let you kill sex workers, the constant bombardment of violence and sexual imagery numbs young minds and makes it seem more acceptable. I'm sure Morgan is wishing she had made some different choices in her life from wherever she is now."

～ ～ ～

"AAAAAAAAAAAAAAAaaahhhhhhhhhhhhhhhhhhhh." A high pitched scream echoed off the pillars and marble floors of the hall. Forseti had fallen asleep on his throne and was startled awake, joining the screaming as his mind attempted to catch up with the stimulus.

"That clumsy bitch!" a woman's voice carried to the throne before another squeal, this one more frustrated than afraid. Forseti rose and peered around his hall, in the dark he could make out a figure laying on its back in the middle of the room, one hand on its neck, the other grabbing a clump of hair. Once the figure was finished yelling it sat up and began to look around. "The fuck?"

"Umm... Hello?" Forseti said before the screaming began anew. He lit the room dimly, his godly essence controlling the braziers and the pillars reflecting the light around the room. He could see the woman now. Dressed in black with light red hair, the woman seemed afraid and disoriented. "It's okay. I'm not sure who you are, but I'm Forseti, this is my hall. Did you wander in from outside, were you recently awakened?"

"Forseti? The meme guy? Is this a joke? Where's the cameras?"

"You know of me? What's a camera?"

"Can it, asshole. Where are we? Hospital? I didn't die, just passed out from the shock?! Yes!" Then with a bit more energy she got up and looked around more. "What kind of hospital is this? Why am I not in bed? Were you taking me somewhere you sick fuck?"

"Hey, I was just sleeping over there until you came in here screaming and writhing on the floor. I'd be happy to help you if you would just tell me who you are, Mrs...?"

"Mrs? I'm not married, why would you assume that."

"Well, I meant no offense. You seem well into childbearing age, I didn't mean to imply you couldn't get a man..."

"Wow. There's a lot to unpack there so we'll back burner it. What is this place, who are you?"

"I am Forseti. This is my home, Glitnir."

"Forseti? The Norse god of judgement, Forseti?"

"Yes! That's me."

"Fuck off. Why the act?"

"Tell you what, obviously something is going on. I can sense that you're Midgardian."

"I'm from Indiana."

"I don't know what that means. Please, come over to this table, perhaps we can figure out what is happening." Forseti led her to the viewing mirror and activated it; if she was surprised by the magic, she showed no indication. He worked with her to find her last known location and they were treated to a horrific scene. Uniformed men and women stood around her lifeless body, taking photos and collecting evidence. In a parking lot nearby, a girl sat crying on the hood of a police car while a woman questioned her.

"So it did happen. I really did die," the woman said numbly.

"I know this is sudden, but people die all the time. They generally don't appear screaming in my house, especially Midgar... erm... Indianans. Any idea why you're in Asgard?"

The woman let out a long sigh and shook her head with realization. "We were making a video, a blood sacrifice to, well... you. I guess we actually sacrificed me."

Forseti looked harder at the woman and then back to the woman on the police car in the mirror. "You're the ones that sacrificed chicken heads! Weird, but I appreciated it. You performed a human sacrifice to me?"

"They weren't really chicken heads. We didn't mean to, but yeah, seems that way. Fuck!"

Forseti stared into the mirror a little longer and eventually closed his eyes and muttered, "Fuck."

That night Forseti sat with Morgan and learned about her, her life, and how she came to be an offering to him. He gave her a room and left her to rest before going to bed himself. The Aesir had outlawed human sacrifice long ago, reasoning that it reduced the number of worshipers, but also unfairly advantaged the gods that preyed on the weak. It was seen as cowardly to encourage someone to die in chains or unarmed, it was far more preferable for them to die in glorious battle with a weapon in hand. Forseti couldn't deny the surge in godly power he felt since waking up and his initial shock wearing off, though. He was as strong as he could ever remember being, his mind was clear and he felt that he had gotten just a bit taller. He would need to decide how to handle the situation with his new charge. She was his responsibility now and he would need to handle it.

Forseti woke in the morning and went to break his fast. He had his usual meal, one of Idunn's apples, a bit of Saehrimnir's bacon and a mug of Heidrun's mead. He checked in on Morgan and found her to still be asleep. Reasoning that dying takes a lot out of someone he went to his back garden and sat to watch the eagles. He enjoyed watching them fly and play, occasionally diving after a rabbit or other small prey that inhabit the tall grasses at his neighbor Vidar's home. As the sun passed mid-day he went to again check on Morgan. She had changed position, but was still asleep.

"Morgan! Are you feeling all right?"

"Hmph? I'mmm wake," she mumbled in reply.

"Are you well? You've been sleeping for quite a while."

"Lemme 'lone. Be up in a minute."

Forseti left her to wake up and sat at the table waiting for her. After another hour he realized she was not waking up and he went again to her room. After a few more rounds of promises to get up he decided ultimately to pull her from bed and carry her to the breakfast table over her protestations. He gave her some of the left-over bacon and a bit of bread. After a quiet meal where Morgan glared at the plate while eating, she began to speak a bit more.

"I had convinced myself it was a dream," she began. "You were pestering me to wake up like my dad always had and I started to believe I was a little girl again at home."

"I'm sorry. I, too, thought this morning that it had been a memory or dream."

"Don't suppose you have coffee?"

"I do not. Tea?"

"Fine." Morgan sat quietly a bit longer before asking Forseti what came next.

"Generally, a servant takes on some of the household chores."

"A what now? Did you just call me a servant?" she asked with eyes now wide awake.

"Well, yeah. You sacrificed yourself to me."

"Not on purpose! If you think I'm going to pop on a maid's outfit and clean this place you are in for a rude surprise. I'm not your momma."

"Nanna."

"I'm not that either!"

"Nanna is my mother. She's not awake yet, still forgotten to your people."

"Oh, sorry. The point still stands, what are we going to do that doesn't involve me being your pet?"

"I've never had a human sacrifice before. The house really takes care of itself anyway. You're welcome to live here and do whatever you want."

"Are there, like, other sacrifices I can hang out with?"

"Afraid any that were ever here faded a long time ago."

"Faded?" Morgan asked, surprised. "What do you mean?"

"When a sacrifice is made, any sacrifice, it transfers power to the god it's intended for. If that sacrifice is a moment of your thoughts or a prayer the energy is fleeting but magnified by many thousands it can sustain us. In the case of a sacrifice of an animal or a person the potential energy from their life is transferred, in other words whatever energy you would have had for your time remaining on earth."

"Okay... so what does that have to do with fading?"

"Your soul was brought here by the sacrifice, but it doesn't exist without cost. The god receiving the sacrifice, in this case me, uses some of the energy, what we call essence, to sustain you. From a strictly academic view it would cost me as much to sustain you for your life cycle as the energy I was granted, or about 75 years. After that it becomes a cost to maintain the servant, or rather, sacrifice. Some gods would dismiss their offerings immediately to retain the essence they gathered."

"What happens to the servant's soul?"

"It's released to Hel," Forseti answered plainly.

"Hell? That's messed up! I didn't sign up for demons and pitchforks!"

"Different Hel. Ours is mostly cold and windy with a lot of wandering around lost."

"That's not better. Man, this is a lot to take in. Pass me one of those apples."

"No can do. Last time we let a Midgardian, err... human, eat one of these it unleashed all the troubles of the world. You must promise me you will never eat a golden apple of Idunn."

"Really? It comes from Idunn? Bit on the nose isn't it?"

"I understand all languages, but I don't know what those words mean in that context."

"We'll work on that. Can I have one of the red apples?"

Forseti nodded and handed her one of Gerda's apples. He also caught sight of a raven peering through his window. "I suppose we can go to Odin's, he'll be expecting us."

"This apple is really good!" Morgan said through lips dripping with juice.

"Gerda's. She's a goddess of the earth and fertility of crops. She will be glad to know you enjoyed it."

"Hey, Forseti?"

"Yes?"

"Please don't dismiss me. Not yet."

15

"I need an ambulance at Oubache State Park, main parking lot!" Megan's voice says over a young man lip syncing, looking frantic.
"While I work on dispatching a unit can you tell me the nature of the problem?" says the dispatcher in the now public 911 call.
"I..." the boy tries to express grief but overacts comedically.
"Ma'am?" The video pans around to the boy's dog, laying in an odd position with head hanging off the couch, but clearly panting.
"I think... I think I killed my best friend."

Kuhlr talk, user Benny80085, 437 likes

The pair walked towards Gladsheim a bit slower than Forseti would normally walk. Morgan found herself enjoying the view and stopped frequently to admire the scenery. She talked to the friendly squirrels that ran along the path and even a deer that came a bit close hoping for the apple core she now carried, which she was glad to give.

"This is awesome. You live like this all the time?"

"Not all the time. There's always a battle around the corner, a trial to hold, worshipers seeking guidance, a scavenger hunt, that kind of stuff." Forseti responded.

"I'd be perfectly happy to sit and play with the animals."

"Just don't be too trusting, they can be real gossips."

"Really?" Morgan asked, confused.

"Yeah. I told you, we understand all languages. That includes animals, or at least the idea of what they're trying to express. If you do encounter one that talks your language, it's probably a shape shifter and I definitely wouldn't trust it."

"Shape shifter? Like Loki?"

74

"You know of Loki?"

"Yeah, trickster god. I think he's related to Thor?"

Forseti snorted. "No, not related to Thor. He's a Jötunn, a Giant. Yes, he is a shapeshifter as are many of his kind."

They soon arrived at Gladsheim and made their way up the steps. Forseti noticed the quiet around them despite the others that were milling around the stairs. He caught some stealing glances and more than a few hushed whispers. Morgan thought nothing of it. They entered the hall walking alongside each other and found themselves the center of attention, with a path in the crowd leading to the thrones. Forseti sighed and walked towards the throne, Morgan following a pace behind, now a bit self-conscious.

"Forseti," Odin said to begin the meeting.

"Allfather." Forseti bowed and signaled to Morgan who also bowed.

"And this is your..." Odin drew out the last word for Forseti to fill in, but Morgan interjected.

"... associate, Morgan. Nice to meet you!"

"Associate," Odin tried the word, but didn't seem to like it. "Forseti, can you tell us how a Midgardian soul came to be your... *associate?*"

Forseti had presided over enough trials to know when a question was leading the conversation down a path. He looked around at many of the assembled gods on their thrones, looking back with interest and confusion. *They've been assembled hastily. Odin hasn't had a chance to tell them what he had only just heard from his spy. Well, the quickest way off the predetermined path is to sidestep it early.* "So good to see all of you! This is the most chairs I've seen filled since my return and it brings a tear to my eye in joy. Odin, what's the occasion? Surely, this isn't just for one so undeserving as myself."

"I asked you a question." Odin reminded him smoothly. Forseti knew that tone, it held back barely contained acid and he also knew Odin's court wasn't as guaranteed to be a fair venue as his own.

"Morgan here was accidentally sacrificed by her friend in a botched offering to me. She died over my altar and so was sent here."

"A *botched* offering?" A nasally voice behind Forseti asked. "You didn't influence it with that mirror of yours? You didn't encourage the behavior in an attempt to gain power? You expect us to believe that suddenly virgins are throwing themselves on the altar for a god they didn't know existed a couple weeks ago?"

"Hey!" Morgan said defensively. She was a virgin, strictly speaking, but she didn't need everyone in the afterlife to know that.

"I did nothing to encourage sacrifices, all of my judgements were over offerings of food. You should know a thing or two about manipulating things though, Loki." Forseti turned to face the tall, skinny man that sat in the last throne. "You've been working for years to keep some gods forgotten and bring others back."

"Enough." Odin growled. "Loki is not on trial here."

"Is this a trial?" Forseti challenged.

"It's an inquiry. We're interested in knowing why there's a sacrificial servant here for the first time in a millennium."

"Then ask my *associate*. I just met her when she showed up, I didn't influence anything."

"I asked you, child!" Odin's eye began to widen and Forseti knew he had overplayed his hand.

"Of course, Allfather. I swear to you I didn't mean for this to happen. I do not have the reach or understanding of the modern world to even attempt such things let alone be successful. I beg the Council's forgiveness for the disruption and breaking of the taboo, though I profess to have done nothing knowingly."

The gods talked amongst themselves and came to an agreement. "Forseti, we accept that the sacrifice was not caused by you, however we must not allow an Aesir or any other god to gain power through sacrifices, as we have long held. To ensure this, you must keep your thrall for 60 more years to offset the essence gained."

"Yes, Allfather. I will do as you command. Thank you for the fair and generous judgement."

After that the inquiry broke apart and the gods went to the banquet table to begin feasting. Many of the group glared at Forseti and Morgan and only a few gave any greeting. Thor came to them and chatted with Forseti as if it were any other day, about what he had hunted that day and the Vanir woman he had met while moving a river. When Thor took his leave Morgan pulled Forseti aside.

"Who was that himbo?" She asked.

"I'm going to need you to write these down because..."

"Ugh. man-bimbo. Pretty to look at, but not a lot going on upstairs."

"Oh. That's Thor."

"You sure? I pictured him differently."

"He spends his days in the wilds so he's a bit scruffy. I think he looks quite a bit more sickly than he used to, he was a barrel of a man in our day."

"Why didn't he look at me or introduce himself or say goodbye? Is it because I'm a woman? That's not cool, man."

"No. It's because you are cattle."

"Excuse me?"

"You're an energy source for us and ultimately you were sacrificed like a common lamb. You have better capacity for language, but we understand actual lambs just fine, too."

"That's... depressing. If we're so expendable, why did Odin punish you for letting me come here?"

"He gave me the equivalent of making me feed you for long enough that I won't benefit from your sacrifice. Like stealing a horse only to be punished by having to keep and raise the horse. "

"Not making me feel any better."

"Take comfort, I was planning to keep you around anyway. You are in tune with the modern people and I need to continue to expand my followers so I'll be remembered and maintain my essence reserves."

"Glad I can be useful to your ego."

"It's not just about ego. If I'm forgotten my energy will dry up and I'll fall asleep until I'm remembered again, if ever. If I'm asleep, I can't maintain you."

They began walking back to Glitnir in silence. After a few minutes Forseti heard sniffles from his companion. "Is everything well?" He asked.

"No," Morgan squeezed out through a tight throat before letting the sob she had been holding back loose. "Everything isn't well. I died, my best friend killed me and now I'm here with a bunch of *gods* and expected to either be a servant for eternity or go wander a cold wasteland!" She sat down on the grass along the road and sobbed a few more moments before continuing. "The only hope I have is my 'master'," she said using air quotes, "and he told me I'm little more than an animal to be slaughtered." Morgan stared at him accusingly through watery eyes as Forseti calmly listened.

Forseti dropped his eyes and frowned before moving to sit down beside Morgan. "I was telling you what they see you as, answering your question. I'm sorry if you interpreted that as how I feel or even that's how all of the gods view humans. I've always admired humans, to have such a short life yet be able to accomplish so much and have so much hope. Your kind builds things that outlast any individual or even any society, the Aesir can go hundreds of years without changing anything including our meals. That bacon you ate has been carved from the same hog since before I was born." Seeing Morgan's scrunched up nose he corrected himself. "Not like that. He dies each day and is butchered only to be reborn the next morning."

"So his fate is to be born, immediately get killed and butchered, then born again?"

"Yes! And we honor him for his sacrifice. Saehrimnir feeds all the soldiers in Valhalla and the Aesir, his sacrifice will keep us strong for the fight at Ragnarok."

"But you still slaughter him each day."

"Well, yes. I see your point, but the point I'm trying to make is I *don't* see you as a sacrificial animal. I understand that it is only through the energy that humans expend on us, whether through worship, offerings, or just thinking about us while watching a video, that keeps us alive. I've been forgotten, I slept a thousand years with no one remembering me until a child reminded the world. One person, not yet of age to birth her own children, made enough of a difference to bring me back. That is why I admire humans and am happy to have one as my *associate*." He said the last word with a smirk and Morgan snorted.

"Thanks. Also, are you talking about Ava? She's, like, 13-years-old, dude. Why bring up child birthing?"

"Only to say she is not yet even an adult. Soon she will have her blood and be married off, but she is already changing the world!"

"We have a lot of things to cover when it comes to... everything that's different than your weird and gross time."

"Does this have to do with you still being a virgin?"

"Why does everyone keep assuming that?"

"Because you were sent here. If you weren't you would not have been deemed a worthy sacrifice."

"Jesus..."

"He's not here, that's a totally different pantheon."

"Wait, so multiple pantheons exist?"

"Yeah, it's all about belief. We had some run-ins with those guys when they were taking over our territory and integrating us into their religion. A bunch of goddesses got split apart, poor Oestre even lost her rabbits in the separation."

Morgan moved her mouth wordlessly a few times before shaking her head to clear it. "Getting sidetracked. So you guys define virgin as someone who hasn't slept with the opposite sex right?"

"No, there's plenty of same sex couplings here. We use penetration as a baseline consideration."

"Oh, okay then. I guess I see where the technicality falls. By penetration you mean..."

"Fingers are fine, I believe you refer to that as 'third base'?"

"That one? That is the idiom you know?"

"I've been watching the mirror a lot. Turns out when some people appeal to a god they aren't always asking for anything."

"Oh, God."

"Exactly."

They sat in silence a little longer. Forseti stared out over the landscape while Morgan looked at her shoes. She sniffled a few times and wiped her eyes. After a heavy breath she looked at him and said evenly, "I wasn't good at telling people what I was feeling when I was alive. I want to be better at that here and since it appears most of you are either assholes or too self-absorbed to notice other people's feelings I think I need to be direct. Is that okay with you?"

"Of course."

"Good. When you explained why Thor didn't acknowledge me you didn't say 'The reason is because *he* viewed you this way', you said it was because I *was* cattle. Then, just now you tried to explain it away as what you meant to say. I'm freshly murdered, in a new place surrounded by powerful beings, and was just told that I can be dismissed without a second thought. I stood up to the Allfather to assert myself as an individual, but I was still scared and then you demeaned me and just a bit ago tried to gaslight me. That hurt. I guess part of me was looking to you for support or as a protector and I realize that isn't fair to you because I put that on you, but I need to know what this relationship is going to be so I don't keep getting disappointed. What do you want from me? Am I going to be doing your dishes until your sentence is over and you can dismiss me or what?"

Forseti stared at this young woman, broken by the events she had endured over the past day, but still strong enough to assert herself to Odin and confront her master. He had a feeling if he did order her to do chores it wouldn't go smoothly for him. "No. I don't need you to do chores. You're welcome to stay at Glitnir as long as you want, but you are my guest. You sacrificed your life to me, even if unwillingly, and I believe that should be repaid with kindness and respect. I take my role as the god of judgement seriously, and I would deem taking advantage of someone in need as a, what did you call it, asshole move?" Morgan barked a laugh and her tension eased. "What I need is what I said earlier. I need someone who can help me understand the world I now find myself in and can keep me relevant. If you can help me with that I swear to you as long as I have the essence to stay awake, or you request to be dismissed, you will have a place here. What do you say, associate?"

"FML. Why didn't I just go to work? All right, fine. Let's get to it." Morgan stood and stared into the sky for a moment before looking down to Forseti, still sitting.

"First question, what is FML?"

16

Jinjer's song Pisces plays over the video, the image showing a Bible laid on a table. The sweet, melodic vocals start.

I drew a different reality, With unconditional loyalty, Ego hardly can be piqued, 'Cause I'm selfless

As the tempo of the song picks up the view shifts to a newspaper showing a headline of Morgan's death. The vocals come back in, harsh and aggressive.

Scale armor blaze, Virgin innocence, One being brings life, Another runs for death

The subtitle to the video reads "Prayers for the impressionable youth".

Kuhlr talk, user TheThompsons82702, 12,570 likes

"So does this thing get internet?" Morgan asked, staring into the viewing mirror as Forseti doom scrolled through negative interviews by focusing on use of his name on earth.

"Is that the thing where people can talk anywhere?"

"You *are* learning!" Morgan said with sarcastic glee.

"No. It doesn't get internet."

"Bummer. You'd think gods would be able to get online."

"Would you?" Forseti glanced up at her.

"Well, yeah. We're used to thinking about gods like they're incredibly powerful and could see everything. There's no easier way to creep on people than the net."

"Hmph."

"Why so mopey?"

"It's nothing."

"That's how we're going to run this partnership? Communication bro, let it out. A few people saying bad things hurting your feelings?"

Forseti sighed and stared at the edge of the mirror, not willing to look up nor ignore Morgan and look into the viewer. "It's not the humans, not completely. The other gods."

"What about them? I thought they passed judgement and now you're good."

"That wasn't judgement, it was punishment. They couldn't find me guilty of any crime or show that I didn't live up to my word, but Odin still needed to show I was being punished. Why in front of everyone though? The Council sure, but the others? Maybe I'm letting something Loki said get to me."

"The guy famous for lying?"

"This was different. Loki would play tricks and tell lies, of course, but what he said rings true."

"The best lies do," Morgan said. "You can't come out telling your parents you're heading to bible study when you're really going to make out with your friend's brother. You tell them you're going to your friend's house, which is true, but left out that she was at bible study."

Forseti glanced up for a moment. "That's a valid point. It's the piece of the restraints that have been bothering me though. These were made to hold a man so powerful that when he fought against them he would cause earthquakes, a man that can shapeshift into all kinds of creatures, yet the piece he gave me was shattered. I only know one tool that could have broken those restraints and it belongs to my uncle. So many have accepted that he's back and working for Odin, even after what he did to Balder. Odin once made me wait in his sitting room for 80 years for him to talk to me just to tell me not to drink from his mead reserves. Loki was imprisoned for only 20 years for killing the most beloved of his children. It doesn't make sense."

"So, I brought brownies home from my friend's mom and said she sent them. I just took them from the pantry on my way out. Helps sell the story."

"I'm not sure these things are comparable."

"You've never been a teenage girl," Morgan said dryly. "Can I try to use the viewer?"

"You can try, it needs godly essence to power, but I don't see why you wouldn't be able to." Morgan tried vainly to move and control the scene, but wasn't able to affect it. She grabbed the knife laying along the edge and did as she had seen Forseti do, slitting her hand and dripping a bit of blood onto the surface. "What are you doing! Are you okay?"

"Relax, not the first time. I'm just seeing if it makes a difference, like registering a new user." Morgan found she was able to move the view and began playing around. She clicked her fingers around the edges of the screen in the corners and eventually started dragging her finger from the edges.

"What are you doing?"

"Exploring... Aha!" When she swiped up from the bottom a new panel appeared in front of the world view. Morgan tried to understand the characters, but was unable to do anything. Forseti focused on the panel and changed the language displayed to English. "Thanks. Give me a few minutes here."

Forseti watched her for a bit before realizing his presence wasn't necessary or noticed so he went to his dining room and made some tea. A bit later he was deep in his thoughts when Morgan yelled for him and he went running to see what the urgency was for.

"I knew it, we have a connection."

"I just heard you yelling, I didn't feel anything..."

"No. Internet. We have an internet connection." She smiled as she showed Forseti a panel that looked like many of the devices he had seen when observing humans.

"How...?"

"You said it yesterday, this world is based on belief. Like I said, most humans would think that immortal gods would have broadband or something, especially since you are known because you responded to social media posts, even if you did it like an old man feeding pigeons the underlying mythos is that you watch social media tagging you and respond."

"I would have never thought of that."

"You're not human and you're from literally a thousand years ago. If you did understand modern humans I'd be more worried about the state of humanity. Now look, we can create accounts and watch what people are saying and comment and all that."

"This is useful?"

"You said if I earned my keep I got to stay. I can teach you the ways of humanity for years, but you'd still not be human and we'd miss this window of clout. Now I can influence directly on your behalf."

"And what, tell people you're a dead servant to the god they've been praying to and they should make more offerings?"

"Gods no, you Norse never were known for your subtlety. Leave that to me. First though, you need to see some of the things that are going on." Morgan pulled up a video sharing site and typed in Forseti's name, the majority of trending results discussing Morgan's death and the dangers of social media. A subset of videos, though, were focused on the danger of vigilantes using paganism to seek justice instead of trusting the police and government, some even going so far as to call Forseti a "false flag" to get children groomed for demon worshiping. One video criticized the American President for not taking a firmer stance on "alternative justice" and challenged his understanding of the younger generation and their "gateway drugs".

"They talk openly about their leader that way?" Forseti asked.

"Yeah. Freedom of speech, it's like the first thing we did when we became a country, made sure everyone could talk shit. The second thing we did was let everyone have weapons for when people talked too much shit."

"In our time that man's tongue would be cut out and he'd be set in the public square as an example."

"In our time he'll get a million likes and an invitation to CPAC. Now let me do my thing here, I have to create some accounts. Are you planning to go by the dining hall at all? I could go for some more of those sweet rolls."

Apparently dismissed, Forseti would make his way to Gladsheim, but took a long walk along the houses first. He mourned his friends that had not yet reawakened and he took pity on those that while awake hadn't regained enough strength to rejoin the others. His own father, Balder, had made his way back to the festivities. Forseti's recent notoriety had seemed to result in a halo effect that gave Balder strength as the story became more well known. Walking up to Balder's home, Breithablik, he saw that the debris was beginning to clear away as the building mended itself. "Father?" Forseti called out.

"I'm here! That you, son?"

"Who else would call you 'Father'?"

"That a way to speak to your elder?"

"Sorry." Forseti glanced down. "Morgan must be wearing off on me."

"Ah, the servant girl. A lot of chatter that caused after you left," Balder said conspiratorially.

"Did it? What kind of chatter?"

"Oh, you know, wondering if you did it on purpose and speculation about how you regained your strength so fast. You have to admit, you've gone from being completely Forgotten to one of the healthiest Aesir in a short time. What should they think?"

"I didn't encourage this, I can give you my word."

"Look, son, I am not of the mind that you did. The fact that your strength is helping me regain strength too is reason not to question your methods. I'm hoping your poor mother awakes soon, such a shame she got mixed up in all of this."

"Mixed up in what?" Forseti became serious and looked directly at his father.

"Well, you know, being Forgotten and all that. Very little writings of her remained for anyone to remember her after..." Balder trailed off, his eyes widening to show he had nearly said something he wasn't meant to.

"After? After what?"

"After... the Christians destroyed our records," he said uncertainly, as if he didn't know how the sentence would end when he started it.

"Father, what are you hiding?"

"Nothing, put it from your mind. I must still be a bit weak. Please, I need to rest."

"Look at me Balder, is there something you're not telling me, or that you can't tell me?" Forseti knew he was pushing in a way that would seem odd if Balder was, in fact, not hiding anything. *He seems more reactive than confused, like he's looking for an answer that will sate me. He has to know something, there's something I'm not being told and it all comes back to Loki.*

"I... I can't say."

"What do you mean you can't say?! What's going on here and why is it being hidden from me?!" Forseti was on his feet and pacing the room.

"I swore an oath to Odin, I can't say any more!"

Forseti left his father's hall and went directly to Gladsheim to confront Odin. Once inside he realized neither Odin, nor any of the other council, were present. In anger he grabbed a few baked goods and went home, chewing a sweet roll as he stomped.

"Oh good, you're home," Morgan greeted him distractedly. "Did you get me some baked goods?"

Forseti was a bit deflated that she hadn't noticed his purposeful stride and glare as he entered. "Uh, yeah. Here." He handed her the pastry and continued, "Can this internet tell us what happened to me? Why I wasn't remembered like the others on the High Council?"

"It doesn't work quite like that, but I actually wanted to ask you about that. Before I died I researched you, tried to find all I could, to make better content, and there wasn't much. It seems all anyone knows of you is reconstructed from one passage written hundreds of years after you fell asleep."

"One passage?"

"Yeah, look here. I pulled up this article written by Ava's dad, Dr. Harrison

Tillmann, he talks about how nearly everything the world knows about Norse mythology can be traced back to only a couple of sources, all written long after the conversion to Christianity, from spoken stories. He describes it as putting together a complex world using Grimm's fairy tales as a source material."

"Fairies? What do they have to do with it?"

"Forget it. Point is there's very little written info about *any* of the gods. If some monk hadn't gotten interested in history and wrote down the stories he was being told, the world may have completely forgotten you guys."

Forseti sat and absorbed that info for a while. He had known their old texts and altars had been destroyed, but he hadn't realized just how scarce their info had become. *Is this what he meant by getting 'caught up in all of this'?* "The other gods, ones that the Christians also took over, were they destroyed as well?"

"No. The Greeks and Romans are super well known, even to me, and I didn't pay attention in history at all. Egyptians, too. Like, we know some of the Norse gods, but there's a lot of writings and monuments to those other ones."

Did we make a mistake? How did Odin let this happen, after giving his own eye to be able to see what was coming? But, why the secrecy?

"Anyway, I've been working on building a social media presence. I couldn't use my old personal accounts, way too creepy, but I set up new ones. I've already commented on hundreds of posts."

"About me?"

"Bit full of yourself aren't you? No, just innocently commenting and building a presence. Agreeing with what people are saying and being friendly so they follow me back. If I started coming out swinging with 'Forseti's my sky daddy' no one would take me seriously. For now I'm just a young business woman between the ages of 25 and 40 with disposable income."

"You're 19 and I know that's not how business people dress in your time."

"It's the internet, no one is who they say they are. Some of my other shill accounts are middle aged men who love guns, an older Democrat that's still a bit racist, one girl that's pretty confident the earth is flat, and a teenage boy that's really into anime. Speaking of my clothes, I'm glad I died in a really great outfit, like the photos of my body are such a vibe, but where can I get other clothes? This goth stuff gets uncomfortable after a while."

Morgan had taken some time to browse photos of her death scene. They were surprisingly easy to find, one tasteful shot anyway, that showed her body bent backwards over a tree with her neck and head out of view over the curve of the trunk.

Her pale legs showed from under a pleated skirt and ended with a pair of heavy black boots. The flowing and purposefully torn shirt she wore over her leather top hung nearly as long as the skirt. She knew she should be upset at the image, but she couldn't help but think how great her legs looked. The angle and the position she was in also made the girls look great. The photo had been titled "Modern Dahlia" by the internet, which she approved of.

"Goths? I knew the Goths, they didn't dress like that," Forseti quipped. He had come across the fashion trend known as 'goth', the dark and severe style that was popular among some modern humans, including Morgan. He couldn't resist taking a jab at her though and put on his best serious face.

"Are you smirking? Was that an attempt at a joke or did you fart? Do gods fart?"

Forseti sighed. "You said you wanted to ask me something about why I'm not known?"

"Nice avoidance, but yes. It doesn't sound like you know much more than I do though. You have a seat on the High Council and the other gods seem to respect you. I looked up all the other Aesir on the council, there's a lot more written about them. Like I said, there's two main references and each only mentions you once. The rest, there's plenty of stuff. Their wikis are huge. What happened?"

"What do you think I've been stressing over?" Forseti said exasperatedly. "I think Loki targeted my info and erased me. I don't know why or how. I think the other Aesir were involved, or are at least covering for him."

"Literally, one of the only things that are written about you is that your hall was the best seat of judgement and all that left were soothed. That doesn't line up with them letting you burn."

"Then what am I to do?" Forseti said, staring at the ceiling.

"Keep looking for answers and be less emo about it." Morgan shrugged.

"Fuck My Life."

17

"You know, a lot of pundits are making fun of "The Cult of Forseti" and its boat without oars. The thing is, they're missing the point of that story. The point was that these people, lawmakers essentially—like congress, were set adrift without oars, floating without direction. Forseti, using his axe, steered the ship and brought them to land. The allegory is that we need to use our judgement, like an axe, to steer congress in the right direction!"

Kuhlr talk, user FositePriest24, 176 likes

Forseti stood by his viewing mirror, which Morgan had dubbed "Oracle", observing the shifts in his legacy. He had been received almost universally positively at first, though now there seemed to be as many, if not more, using him as a warning against deviation from their cultural norms. The other gods seemed to be avoiding him and Morgan was busy testing the theory that she would maintain her current state regardless of what she consumed. So far she had eaten enough pork and sweet rolls to make even Thor nod in appreciation.

He decided to check in on Ava. His priestess had been quiet since the incident of Morgan's death. He found her in her room watching TV from under her covers. It was a 24 hour news network discussing the latest in the Megan Mays murder case. It appeared Megan had been cooperating with investigators and they were working towards a plea deal. Megan was home on house arrest with mandatory psychological exams and check ins. Ava's father walked into the room.

"You're still watching all of this?"

"Yeah," Ava responded quietly.

"You have to stop dwelling on it. This isn't your..."

Ava cut him off, "She looked up to me! ME! She wanted to emulate what I did with the videos and get recognition."

"You can't control how people respond to you or take the things you say. You never meant to harm anyone."

"Didn't I? I asked a brutal Norse god to punish my bullies! I'm lucky he didn't send lightning bolts!"

"Ava, you don't believe there's really a pagan god out there watching you and waiting to hurt people." Forseti blushed a bit, but didn't blame Dr. Tillmann for his opinion.

"I don't know... I just want things to be normal, I want that girl to not be dead and I want people to stop accusing me of bringing a demon to earth!"

"I know honey, that's just a few vocal loonies though."

"I hear the phones ringing all the time, it's people wanting to talk to me isn't it?"

"Not completely. A good portion are, but your mother and I can handle those. You shouldn't be obligated to speak to anyone about the matter."

"Dad," Ava started, "why were the Norse gods so angry and mean?"

"Well, that's a great question. I'm sure you've seen on your news coverage that most of the major deities were great warriors and the only honorable way for a Nord to die was with a weapon in hand. It's important to remember that these gods were a product of their environment and time. With such few resources and brutal living conditions, the Norse were tough and their gods had to be too. Many wars were fought between clans over food and land, the best way to make sure there's enough food is to eliminate some of the mouths through battle. Obviously going to battle isn't appealing to most, so the mythologies tend to reward those who join battles. If you die of old age, you're going to an eternal life of blandness in Hel, die in 'glorious' battle and you get to go to Valhalla!" Dr. Tillmann stopped to make sure Ava was keeping up with him and not upset over anything he had said yet. She nodded that she was following. "The gods were just as hardcore, constantly doing battle amongst themselves and preparing for a huge, unavoidable fight at Ragnarok.

He stood and walked over to the globe Ava kept on her bookshelf. "Now, Forseti is a god introduced by the Germanic tribes that moved north, hence Norse—North Germanics." He showed the path that the settlers would have traveled into Scandanavia. "He was likely held up as a fair judge of people and events to tame the wilder of the people. Justice is fine, battle is fine, but it has to be done within the rules."

"How is fighting okay?" Ava exclaimed.

"It's not now, but it's unfair to assign modern views on people from a thousand years ago. Now, we can grow crops much more successfully and in more environments, not to mention our infrastructure for travel and shipping. Then, though, their neighbors' stock of chickens might have been the difference between your family living or dying."

"So, they're right? These old gods don't have a place in the modern world."

"Not at all, sweetheart. Yes, the Norse gods are mostly known for being hardcore and that is what's shown in television shows and movies about Vikings, but it isn't the whole story. There's dozens of other gods and goddesses besides the ones that are famous. Frigg, Freyja, and Frey were all fertility and good weather. Balder, Forseti's father, was the god of fairness and kindness and his mother, Nanna, was a goddess of joy and peace. Even Odin was more focused on gaining knowledge than kills."

"Why don't we hear about those?"

"They're not as exciting to modern audiences. Most of the people making entertainment aren't praying for good crops. Science has replaced those needs, so the stories of heroes and battles are what get told. It's the same for any of the old religions, you know more about Zeus and Hercules than about Persephone. Everyone knows about the powerful Roman god Pluto, but not the fair Feronia, the Egyptian Osiris instead of Min..."

"Okay, I get your point." Ava jumped in before the list got in the way of the topic.

"Right. The point being that we look at these stories with a modern lens and try to understand how they were worshiped or what their roles in societies were when really, we don't know much other than what was written down. We can assume, but if future civilizations only have Harry Potter and The Lord of the Rings to go off of, they will make some wild assumptions about us."

Ava stood and made a lap around her small room, stopping to look out a window. "I don't understand how this is supposed to make me feel better about a girl dying."

"It's not. A terrible thing happened, and that is not your fault. The narrative from here though, that's yet to be written. Everyone is looking at this through a narrow perspective, through Forseti, which is a shame. The attention your videos were causing were also doing a lot of good for mythology researchers and gaining attention for an interesting pantheon. If you're not taking credit for all those good things, then you can't take the blame for the bad either."

"Thanks, I guess that makes sense."

"Does it? I lost the thread there after a while."

"I know, but you got back around to it. Can you tell me more about the Norse fertility goddesses?"

It pained Forseti to see Ava, the girl that had brought him back, suffering for what happened. She didn't deserve it, it wasn't her choice or actions that caused the death. *You didn't cause the downfall of the Norse gods, your choices didn't cause Odin to free Loki, so why are you taking it so hard?* Since when did his internal monologue get snarky? He was right though, why was he so sullen over things others were doing? He looked back to Ava, now going through a book of Norse gods with her father. As he flipped the pages Forseti used a bit of influence to make it fall open to the entry on Nanna. *There, you want to know about strong, kind, and loyal women? Start with my mother.* He stood to walk away from the table and turned around to find Morgan in the process of sneaking up on him.

"Gah! Remind me to get you a bell," he said.

"Sorry buddy, I don't go in for collars until after a few dates."

"I'm trusting that is a reference to some kind of deviance."

"Obviously," Morgan retorted. "What are you standing up all purposeful for? You finally giving Oracle a break?"

"Yes, I think I know what I need to do."

"I'm all ears."

"I only see the two."

Morgan sighed. "Get to the point."

"I can't control what the other gods are doing, and if the ones that are here won't talk to me then my objective is easy. Wake up the other gods."

"Just like that?"

"What, like it's hard? Just make a viral thingy for some of them and people will love it and they'll start waking up."

"Just make a viral thingy? That's not how that works, if so every business would have viral content. Right now it's really just Wendy's and Ryan Reynolds that can pull it off consistently."

"Then we start working on it, we have eternity. Whatever is going on, I don't think those that still sleep were part of it, and if it is about me I can't let them keep suffering for whatever I did."

"All right, some of my accounts have already started to ingratiate themselves with groups and showed a little knowledge of the myths so I might be able to get conversations going. Any ideas where to start?"

"Fertility gods and goddesses, especially Nanna and Fulla."

Morgan was staring at Oracle, "I understand Nanna, that's your mom, but why Fulla? Looks like she was mostly a servant to Frigg and took care of her shoe collection."

"Frigg shared much with her and confided in her. She may know information I need."

"The fact that this translation says her name means "bountiful" doesn't affect that decision?"

"Well, erm, we may have had a few..."

"Eww. Stop. I'm on it. Where are you going?"

"To see Odin, I'm giving him one more chance to tell me what's going on before I reopen my court."

"You go, girl," Morgan called after him with a snap of her fingers.

"Odin!" Forseti said loudly as he walked into the hall and saw him sitting at the head of the thrones. A few of the others were nearby, Frigg, Frey, and Balder all in their thrones enjoying their lunch.

"Yes, Forseti? Good day, have you come to dine?"

"No, Allfather. I've come to ask you a question."

"Of course. What can I answer for you?"

"You will answer?"

"If I have the knowledge, of course I will answer."

"Mimir, you witnessed that?"

"I did," a voice said from Odin's belt loop.

"Odin," Forseti began, "what happened when we were Forgotten? Why is Loki running around on Earth for you, destroying my artifacts and all these other's are sworn to keep things from me?"

Odin stared at Forseti, taken aback by his boldness, but he knew he was caught. He had given his word. "Loki is doing my work. Some of that involved destroying records. The others that knew of this plan were told of its importance and the need for silence."

"That didn't answer the question—WHY?!"

"Do NOT raise your voice to me." Odin rose from his seat. "You wish to know why? It's because we're preventing Ragnarok, we're keeping the world alive. You! You and your justice were going to kill us all!"

"How? How do you figure I would bring about Ragnarok? You've seen the end, Loki brings it about and started it when he helped to kill Balder."

"Yes, but why does Loki begin the war?"

"Because he's crazy? Because it was foretold? What reason do you need?"

"Maybe because his punishments became too severe, maybe because he was tired of taking the blame and suffering under the boots of the Aesir."

"It's my fault? Blame the judge?" Forseti could hardly believe what he was hearing.

"His pranks had always been harmless, telling Idunn there were better apples outside the wall and that sort of thing. He began escalating after a few of your trials."

"So... what was the plan? Kill me off?"

"I didn't agree to answer that question."

"It doesn't matter, I'm back. Knowledge isn't confined to a location anymore, it's everywhere. You want me to keep doing whatever it was I was doing to destroy the world? If not, I think you should tell me what the issue is. What's this about being too hard on Loki?"

"The Giants, his people, saw his punishments as attacks on their kind and were getting worked into a frenzy when we trapped him in that cage."

"The Giants? I mean, yeah he's one of them, but he spends more time with Aesir than them, he's hardly representative of them."

"Doesn't matter, he looks like they do and he was born of Jotunheim. They understand justice, but between Thor killing every Giant he comes across that looks "suspicious" and you doling out harsh sentences they see Loki as a symbol of Giant oppression."

"Loki went with Thor to Jotunheim for one of his visits!"

"What aren't you understanding, boy? They're not interested in what Loki has done wrong, only with how the Aesir treat his kind. Your punishment with the snake and his wife was the last straw, I saw it through the well all those years ago. The Giants would rally, Loki's children would lead them and free him from his chains to attack Asgard. We had to appease the Giants, we had to stop the coming war."

"Since when do we shirk from battle and prophecy? We play our parts!" Forseti was shouting now. Ragnarok had been foretold long before his birth, no one worked to avoid it, it was just accepted as surely as the coming sunrise.

"We don't have to! Why do you think I've given all? My eye, my own life on the World Tree, carrying around a dead man's head? All to find a way around Ragnarok, all to save the realms. And we did it."

"By destroying me?"

"Don't be so vain. You may have set things in motion, but none of us were blameless. As I said, Thor is no friend to the Giants and many of us have a long history with them as well. They're uneducated and violent, but poorly martialed. Hel would bring them together and lead them. They would have attacked eventually whether you were around or not, it was a matter of time.

Once we decided to erase you it was a matter of appeasing Hel. We freed Loki and put him to work for us."

"My life for Loki's. That was the trade?"

"I wish it had been that easy. You're a member of the High Council and you were a powerful image to the humans at the time, especially through your Lawspeakers. There wasn't an easy way to make you go away, not without the rest of us."

Forseti looked at the ground, his mind racing. Suddenly his attention snapped to Balder. "That's what you meant by getting caught up in this! You all had to have parts of you erased too to destroy me."

"Yes," Odin brought his attention back to him. "So much of our writings had to be destroyed, our followers given a new story to tell. I viewed the futures many times through the well, and the path was a twisted one. To stop Ragnarok, all of the Aesir had to be Forgotten. Loki made contact with some of the Christians on Earth and worked out a deal—he'd give them our territories if they allowed our worshipers to keep some of their traditions. Just enough to remember the old stories and tell them to their children.

"Over time the stories became legends and Loki began influencing scholars at the time to write the stories down and tell them afar. Not long after, I awoke here on my throne. Mimir was already awake, apparently he had never gone to sleep. Loki had remained awake as well, able to keep himself sustained on the relationships he had built. Over the years, more awoke, and Loki continued to spread our stories. Turns out, a couple of the stories floating around mentioned you, albeit briefly so we never noticed it. The altar though, that was unexpected."

"So now what?" Forseti asked, exhausted and heartbroken, "Now what do we do? I'm here."

"Yes, that's exactly what we've been trying to figure out. The Giants don't seem to be too riled up about it, though they aren't in much more strength than most of us. I believe that the window for Ragnarok has closed, though I must insist that you consult us before issuing punishments to any Giants in the future."

"I'll keep that in mind," Forseti said dryly. "Maybe consult me before possibly dooming an entire race of godly beings to extinction?"

"I'll keep that in mind."

Forseti left the hall quickly, returning to his home to find Morgan on Oracle. "Time to earn your keep."

"Okie dokie. What's up?"

"I know why there's so little info about us, the gods were stupid. We need to fix it."

"Okay, is this what you feel like when you can't keep up with me?"

"We're going to bring them back. All of them, the Forgotten. We're going to get them awake and let the world know who the Norse gods were."

"Cool. I'm in. Where are you going?"

"To get the hall set up, it's time to reopen the court."

18

"So..." Forseti droned as his mind tried to keep up with the torrent of information Morgan was giving him. "The other gods have had years, decades even, of influence?"

"Yeah." Morgan confirmed.

"And these *movies* and books and *dolls*? They've had this... platform to tell our stories?"

"I don't know about that. I can show you when the Norse mytholo... *stories*," she caught herself, "began to gain traction. The basics, like Odin, Thor, and Loki have been in history books and stuff forever, but 70 or so years ago people started writing about them again. The comic books inspired kids who grew up to write more books and make movies. The other stories, the Greeks and Romans, have always been big hits so it makes sense that you guys blew up too."

"But they only discussed certain gods?"

"Yeah, what I considered the major gods until I found out about you."

They were looking into Oracle, browsing the internet for images and info on the other gods. Forseti had accepted that the other gods tried to erase him and was hoping to use his newfound strength to punish them, though now he wondered how much power they had accumulated over the time he slept. He could trace a pretty clear line through the rise of popularity in their stories, and he had to assume Loki had influenced or inspired certain stories to be told, though he still didn't understand how Loki had remained awake when even the strongest Aesir had slept. He knew Loki was clever and patient, and he knew he was convincing. It was no wonder over the course of centuries he had been able to construct the stories he wanted the humans to tell. *If it hadn't been for that one altar...*

"You know," Morgan started, "I still don't get why they did what they did. I know you think you told me, but can you explain it like I'm five?"

Forseti sighed. "Loki killed Balder, which was the first sign of Ragnarok."

"Which is the end of the world?"

"Mostly. A few survive and build a new world."

"And you guys know this because Odin tossed his eye into a well?" Morgan asked doubtfully.

"No! That was for divine knowledge. This was told to him by a prophetess."

"So... you guys knew it was coming?"

"We did." Forseti answered, nodding his head. "Frigg tried to protect him. She went to every living creature and plant in the realms and had them swear they'd never harm him. All but the mistletoe, a young and weak thing that she didn't think would be able to harm him."

"How'd Loki figure that out?"

"He disguised himself and asked Frigg if all had sworn."

"And... she answered?" Morgan stared with a fair bit of judgement. "You all know he can shapeshift, you knew he would be a key player in Ragnarok, and you keep falling for that?"

"Millenia are long, we make mistakes. Anyway, we found Loki and punished him."

"Yeah yeah, cave and snake and other horrors, skip that."

"The Giants became agitated at our judgement. Loki's wife, Sigyn, was well loved among their people and they didn't like seeing her paying for Loki's sins." He explained.

"She got herself into that mess and married a jerk. Why would the average Giant care?"

"So I thought. Turns out fear and uncertainty can be harnessed more easily than logic. Their daughter, Hel, gained quite a bit of influence during that time. She encouraged their anger, redirected it against the Aesir instead of the one who had truly done wrong. Ragnarok was coming, we all knew it."

Forseti got quiet and stared at the wall for a moment. Morgan sat patiently and waited, she knew he had been hurting, but wanted to fully understand the situation. He had alternated between hours of sullen silence, sitting in his throne, and manic effort to arrange his hall. These moments were interspersed with angry ranting and naps, making Morgan realize that gods weren't all that different from stressed out teenagers.

"This is where you lose me," she said quietly. "If you knew it was coming, why couldn't you stop it? Why let Loki hang around, why keep his giant wolf-child here that will kill Odin, why give Hel dominion over the dead and therefore an army, why let everyone play a game where they try to hurt Balder with spears? I feel like there were a lot of questionable decisions."

"We're Norse. Life is hard, and we endure many trials and suffering. Like any true Norse we face those challenges, we don't shy away. What message would it send to our followers if we backed out of a fight? If we faced death with anything other honor, with our weapons in hand? We live our lives and come what may."

"Uh huh," Morgan grunted. "Except, the lead god, your grandfather, was obsessed with finding a way to avoid it and apparently did."

"Yes. So it would appear. We knew he sought to change the minds of the Norns, to stop the inevitable. For most of us it was a humorous quirk, never thought to have a chance of success. I, for one, didn't think he would determine *me* to be the problem. We didn't think that he'd go as far to destroy the gods in order to appease and delay the Giants."

"The guy that hung himself for nine days so he could understand some runes? It didn't occur to you he might go to any lengths to succeed?"

"You've been doing more research than you let on." Forseti said with a sharp tone.

"Well, you haven't exactly been chatty these past few days so I had to go looking on my own. Do you think Ragnarok can happen now?"

"I don't think so. Most of the Giants are Forgotten, and a thousand years is a lot of time to cool the animosity. Plus, Balder's back now and Loki's free."

"So what's the issue? We can all just relax and stuff, right?"

"No," Forseti said sadly. "No. Too many of my people still sleep and the world below needs to hear our stories. I've been researching too, you know? The land you come from, it's just as troubled as any I've seen and your people have forgotten how to be a proper society. Odin, Allfather or not, must answer for his choices. There's work to be done yet."

"Then let me show you what I've been working on." Morgan stood and walked across the room. Torn on whether to follow her and let her get away with ordering him around or sating his curiosity, Forseti begrudgingly stood and walked slowly after her. When he arrived at Oracle he saw a waterfall of posts and comments that Morgan had explained amounted to a conversation in the chaotic world of the internet. "I reactivated some of my older accounts that no one knew were mine, that way not every account I'm using shows as being new."

"Why would you have accounts where people didn't know who you were?

Isn't the point to talk with friends and like-minded people?"

"Oh, sweet, innocent Forseti. That's what all the sites say, and some people even use them that way, but the majority of accounts on some of these sites are fake people, ingratiating themselves and subtly, or not so subtly, directing conversations or influencing people's opinions. Sexually frustrated teens invented it, governments perfected it."

"What does sex... never mind, carry on."

"So I've been putting these accounts to use. One was a fan-fiction writer with quite a following, she's been writing a series of Forseti stories." Morgan looked up suddenly and said seriously, "Don't read those." Looking back to the screen, she pulled up a site with artistic renderings of gods. "This account is a guy that was obsessed with K-Pop stars and drew pics of them shirtless, now he's put out a few special edition Forseti images."

"Those don't look anything like me."

"So? People just have to think about you, right? Besides, that weird page-boy haircut isn't going to get anyone's juices flowing."

"What is wrong with my hair? Near every man had this style in the late 900's"

"The issue is that you have bangs. You've been watching people, get a haircut that's more modern."

"Like this?" Forseti thought a moment and his hair style changed. The thick waves on the side thinned out, the bangs growing to a similar length. Forseti pulled a ribbon from seemingly nowhere and tied the top layers back in a messy, wavy ponytail, the under layers still falling around his shoulders. When he pulled the hair back Morgan saw he had grown a beard as well. Morgan stared with her mouth open for a long moment until Forseti got a bit nervous, "Well? This is what the modern Viking representations look like. Is it all right?"

"Yeh, uh, yeah! Yeah, it's... it's good. Makes you look like a completely different person. How'd you do that?" Morgan hoped that her question would divert attention from the blush she could feel warming her cheeks.

"Immortal being composed of thoughts and prayers. I can't change my bone structure or anything without the beliefs of followers, but things like hair and clothes are easy enough."

"Well, I'll adjust the artwork accordingly. I didn't really draw these, I stole them from another site and made a few changes. The big effort is focused over here though." She returned to the view that had been up when they approached. "This is FollowMe. It's a running thread of topics that people post and then others can discuss it in the comments. Everyone's here, unlike Kuhlr which is mostly young people and old people that still think they're young. This is our window to the mainstream, I have about 30 accounts working on discussing politics, criminal justice, and eventually—you. They've been picking up followers at a pretty good clip, if I assume about half the followers are other trolls or bots, we're still making some headway. Even if the other fakes pick up the thread and run with it we'll accomplish the goal."

"Which is?"

"Keep people talking about you. If I have my way you'll be a lightning rod for debate. We've already seen it to some extent with the news agencies, I think we can lean into that a bit more. In fact, I'm banking my existence on it. I know you also want to give a platform for the other Forgotten. I've been working on that too. Actually, you're little priestess was already a step ahead of me."

"Ava?"

"Yeah. She's been using her following to educate people on the other Norse gods, the less brutal ones. She just finished a series of interviews with a Norse expert in a cowboy hat from Colorado discussing the origins of a bunch of the goddesses. It was good, do you think Freyja would be up to hanging out with me? She sounds pretty awesome." At a confused look from Forseti she continued, "She's also made sure to bring you up in a peaceful light, focusing on your role as a fair judge, not a bloodthirsty conqueror. She lost some followers early on, but she's starting to grow again with a different following, but not totally. A lot of the casual followers, I'm talking thousands, have stayed around and are engaging with the new content. I've been inserting myself in the comments to keep the flames stoked, asking questions I know the answers to so someone will answer and tell a cool story or something. The internet loves to explain things, and then argue about the explanations, so really it's not hard to get them talking. Then I make references to something I read, that another of my accounts posted, and it becomes a big self-referential discussion where I control the path."

"Morgan... I think you frighten me."

"Not the first time I've heard that."

"How did you come up with all of this?" Forseti asked.

"I don't have anything else to do and I grew up on the internet. It's not much different from what troll farms do."

"Have they escaped Jotunheim?"

"Umm... no? Different kind of troll I assume. We mean it as someone who makes things up on the internet for attention. You have trolls?"

"Yeah. They're Giants, just tend to live with their families alone and not in the larger towns. They're a bit stand-offish, but not so bad."

"Anyway... You told me to do this like my afterlife literally depended on it so I'm giving it my all."

"You're a good person, Morgan. You don't deserve what happened to you."

"Yeah well, I wasn't doing much with it down there," she pointed to the screen. "Might as well give it a fresh start and try to change the world."

"A fresh start..." he mumbled to himself. "Hey, let's see about getting you some new clothes!"

"Where?"

"We'll talk to Frigg. She's the goddess of weaving."

"Can't you just, like, make clothes appear?" Morgan asked.

"Do you want me designing and fitting your clothes? Even making them with essence I need to know what I'm making."

"Uh, no. Let's go ask the queen of the gods to make me some clothes, I guess." Morgan started walking along with Forseti who seemed a bit eager to go. "Hey, are you just using this as an excuse to see that, erm... bountiful attendant of hers? She's been popular on the fan art sites and I heard she had returned."

"I don't know what you're talking about." Forseti answered as he walked briskly down the path. "Where would you hear that from anyway? You don't talk to anyone else."

"You talk in your sleep." Morgan smirked.

"Lady Frigg." Forseti bowed as he approached Odin's consort. "I've come to request your expertise."

"Grandson, it is good to see you. Our last meeting was unfortunate, and I'd be glad to help put it behind us. How can I assist you?"

"My charge, Morgan here, only has the clothes she died in and would be grateful for other options. I have no talent for these things and would be honored to be able to gift her your creations."

"Hmmm..." Frigg looked Morgan over. "Yes, I think that can be arranged. Tell me, Morgan, do you favor such elegant yet severe styles or would you like to explore other fashions?"

Morgan, a bit taken aback by Frigg's willingness to help and not prepared for the question, stuttered. "Yeah. I mean, yes, ma'am. I like this style, but I will gladly defer to your taste and recommendations." She had picked up on Forseti's formal and respectful tone and wasn't sure which of the gods could fry her with their minds yet so followed suit.

"Forseti dear, would you give us some time?" Frigg asked.

Forseti looked to Fulla, who was sitting behind the thrones with other attendants. "Yes, my lady." Forseti went to Fulla and greeted her before asking her to step aside to somewhere more private.

19

"All right people, let's get into places and quiet on the set!" an assistant shouted. The noise in the cavernous studio dropped quickly as the builders and other stagehands stopped their work and made their way to the food table. On the set, a small bedroom and a cut in half living room were lit, and two young women walked to their places.

"Now remember," the director called out, "you've just gotten home from the BDSM club and found the letter that your film was rejected from being entered in the Indiana Film Festival. You're desperate to become famous and are trying to figure out what to do next when the idea comes to Megan."

"I don't remember any of that from the news articles," the shorter actress, who played Megan, responded.

"Doesn't matter, creative liberty for entertainment. Now look, I have three days to get this thing in the can before my next project starts so let's get to it. If you guys could amp up the repressed lesbian attraction that would help sell the scene."

As the actresses went through their lines and another crew prepared their gear to head into the woods for tomorrow's shoot, a tall figure stood with a group of producers and watched.

"I've never seen a script and crew come together so fast to capitalize on a current headline," a balding man remarked.

"Well, luckily, I had some writers without a project currently to work on it," the taller man, wearing snakeskin boots and a brown suit, said. "You'll be first to get this story out there, even before the trial gets underway!"

"Are we sold on this being idol worshipping and intentional?" The other man is a bit taller than the balding man, but still a foot shorter than the man in a suit.

"Paul, who's your primary audience here?" the man in a suit asked.

"Generally, women between 34 and 70," Paul responded.

"They'll attack this like piranhas on a cow. It has everything they're looking for, demon worship, lesbians, punishment for those things and in the end a heartwarming message about the importance of family."

"Well, you haven't steered us wrong yet Mr. Laufison," the balding man interjected. "I think we can have this edited and ready to air by end of month."

"Good to hear. I have another meeting to get to, call if you have any issues." The man in the suit, Luca Laufison, dismissed himself and headed to the car waiting for him. The latest scion of the Laufison family had a full day of production meetings and investor calls to attend to. His company, Thokk Entertainment, has been a pillar of Hollywood since its inception along with television and print investments.

While the young CEO was known to keep a low profile and limited availability, as seemed to be a family trait, the company could always be relied on to be invested in pop culture touchstones, producing content in a variety of formats, or providing funding for up and coming projects. Luca's next stop would take him to their news holdings.

៚ ៚ ៚

"Welcome back," Daisy Dunn said from her studio. She was sitting in a firm armchair angled towards a coffee table along with a man, who occupied an identical chair on the other side of the table. Coffee mugs half filled with cool water sat in front of them. "This is The Final Word with Daisy Dunn, and we're here with Freedom First News correspondent Doug Hatcher. Tonight we're diving deeper into the twisted phenomenon of occultic worship by liberal extremists in an attempt to cause harm to good people. Doug, I know we've discussed this Cult of Forseti before, especially after the ritual murder that happened in Indiana, on both of our shows, what has changed since those events?"

"Thanks for having me, Daisy," Doug said. "We've been talking for years about the cabal inside the beltway that's grooming children and working against the interest of honest Americans, and now their blinded followers are enacting the most evil part of their plan yet—an attack on Christian faith by supplanting it with false gods. What could be more beneficial to them than a population of pagan worshipping voters that will do their bidding? A few paid actors put out some allegedly funny videos showing staged acts of divine retribution and these sheep eat it right up and perpetuate the narrative!"

"Old news though, Doug! We've established and proven that weeks ago and our viewers are certainly smart enough to see through the tactic, but I believe some new information has come to light that we're ready to break right here on The Final Word."

"You're right, Daisy. It pains me to say this, but we were leaked a thumb drive discovered by a computer technician in Michigan who asked for anonymity for his own safety." Doug looked towards the camera directly now, turning slightly in his seat. "On this hard drive is files, including a list of names titled 'Needs Punished' and assorted news articles and files detailing their alleged crimes. The images coming across your screen are heavily redacted to protect the victims, but we are working with authorities on what we believe to be a conspiracy to cause harm or death to these citizens outside of the legal system."

"Unbelievable." Daisy wrinkled her nose and looked at Doug with anger creased brows. "Is there any pattern to the names or other evidence to suggest why these names are on that drive?"

"We can't be sure, but the names of some prominent conservative politicians as well as accused criminals awaiting trial are included. The drive itself bears a football shaped marking from a pen, which we know is a rune commonly associated with the Forseti Cult." Doug shook his head a bit and frowned into the lens.

"We warned just last week this would be the logical escalation of the vigilante justice that people are asking for on social media. It may seem harmless and innocent, but every video gives more legitimacy to these sick elites. I'm sickened, Doug, I really am. First, it's pizza used as a cover to traffic children, now Kuhlr videos to desensitize Americans to ritual sacrifice and encourage mob behavior. When do good, decent, Americans stand up and say, 'Enough is enough, I'm not some pawn for you to play with?'"

"Well, all I can say, Daisy, is for our viewers to be vigilant and standby. It's going to get hotter before we fix it and we'll be bringing more as we uncover the files on this drive. If you see someone sharing these videos you need to downvote and comment to discourage the behavior. Every time you click past one, you're saying it's okay for the maker to pervert our brave police and justice systems..."

∽ ∽ ∽

In a contemporary and stark office in Indianapolis, Megan Mays sits with her parents and her legal team. The lawyers and assistants present are young but have years of experience. They had approached Megan soon after her arraignment and convinced her to fire her public defender and allow them to represent her pro bono. They had been honest. They were an assortment of junior and senior associates from large law firms that had started their own firm and were looking to make a name for themselves. Megan's case would be a huge publicity opportunity for them if they won. Megan liked the pitch, it meant they'd be desperate to win. Her parents added that they had to be better than a free public defender. Today, they were discussing their strategy and preparing for the upcoming trial.

"We need to make sure we're always aware of the public perception," a woman was lecturing. "Every eye roll and smile will get talked about, remember how much people were analyzing the Amber and Johnny trial. We'll also need to approve the outfits you'll be wearing to court ahead of time, if you could send us some pics of options."

Megan was struggling to focus on the conversation. She didn't want to think about outfits, she didn't want to discuss her posture and listening attentively and all that stuff. She wanted to go back to bed, she wanted to hide under her covers and shut the world out and try to forget about how badly she missed her friend. She knew there were reporters outside her house and knocking at the door occasionally. She knew news networks were talking about her, she had overheard her parents discussing it. Her parents had been great about protecting her and giving her room back, they had even gone to her apartment and cleaned it out so she wouldn't have to go back there again. *I hope Morgan's parents are doing okay...*

"Megan?" The woman interrupted her thoughts. "I know it's hard to talk about this and break it down so clinically. I know it still hurts, but we need you to be present. We're here to help you." She wasn't unkind or condescending, she looked genuinely concerned and understanding.

"Yeah," Megan croaked through a dry mouth. "I know... Sorry."

20

"Happy Friday everyone and welcome back to Entertainment Today." A morning show host says through polished teeth. "If you, like millions at home, caught last night's premier of *Kuhlr Cult*, you may need a bit more coffee since you likely didn't get much sleep."

"I know I didn't." His co-host added as she sipped white wine. "What a disturbing story, especially knowing it's based on real life."

"It is, yeah. I'm sure many of our viewers know about the Morgan Green tragedy, which, by the way, jury selection starts for today. It's a great behind the scenes look at events leading up to the tragedy as told by friends and classmates of the girls involved."

"A bit later in the show we'll be talking to the executive producer of the film, who we have to disclose is a part owner of our own network and get his take on the film and the events that inspired it. But, first let's welcome our next guest, Bindi the Lemur!"

〜 〜 〜

"Hey, boss!" Morgan said cheerfully as she came out for breakfast.

"You're awfully energetic this morning. Sleep well?" Forseti asked.

"I did, but for some reason I just feel refreshed, charged up today. I don't know how to explain it, like electricity in my veins."

"Electricity, huh? I feel a bit powered up today too. I assumed it was a good night of social media."

"But that wouldn't do anything for me, would it?" Morgan asked, pausing from putting bacon onto her plate.

"Well, sure it would. You're a spirit that lived on after death, here in our realm. The same rules apply, if people are talking about you, remembering you, expending any energy whatsoever, you reap a piece of that energy. It means lower cost for me to keep you here too."

107

"So, I'm, like, a goddess?"

"Something like that. There's a lot of ways of looking at being a god, and from your use you mean it as a deity, like being a god of *something*. In your case, it's more being sustained by the energies of others. The only real difference is that you actually lived, existed. We were born purely from the will of the humans who were looking to explain the natural world so are associated with different phenomena," Forseti explained.

"So... in short I'm a goddess?"

"Yeah, I'd say..."

"Fuck yeah! I told Tyler I was in junior high and he called me a weird Wiccan."

"Tyler..." Forseti was taken aback and confused.

"Old boyfriend," Morgan said dismissively. "I told him he should treat me like the goddess I was, he decided Rachel from the field hockey team was an easier skirt to get into."

Morgan walked off from the kitchen full of excitement and energy. Forseti watched after her as she left, wondering what new events had led to this surge. He finished his fruit and went to Oracle to investigate.

"Morgan, we need to talk," Forseti called towards her room after spending some time catching up on the previous day's events.

"What's up?" Morgan emerged in one of her new outfits that Frigg had made her, though Forseti noticed the skirt was quite a bit shorter than it had been before, and the top seemed a bit more filled out.

"Do you feel any different? Have you noticed any changes to yourself?"

"Yeah, actually. My boobs got a little bigger, I think. Also, my hair got darker, more like its dyed color than my natural."

"Anything else?" Forseti prompted.

"Just a constant buzz of energy coming in, like I drank too much coffee. I think it's making me... feel horny? That's weird, I'm sorry. I haven't been exactly in the mood since dying, but now I just want to go find Thor or Freyja and ask them to tie me up."

"First things first, don't have sex with Aesir. Or Vanir. Or Giants. I'd really just recommend avoiding any of the gods, you don't want to experience godly childbirth."

"But if it's another goddess..."

"Morgan, my great, great grandfather was brought into the world by a space cow licking an ice cube. Heimdall was birthed simultaneously by 9

108

mothers who were also sisters and there was no father. The rules are a bit different." Forseti gently grabbed Morgan by her shoulders to try and focus her on what he was saying. "More importantly, remember how we were talking about how your energy is coming from the thoughts of the humans?"

"Yeah, that was like an hour ago."

"And do you remember when I explained that for gods, much of who we are is what we are perceived to be by those feeding us those energies?"

"Kind of. That one's still a bit confusing."

"No! It's not!" Forseti shook her a bit as her eyes grew wide. "You understood it when we had the conversation, you're very smart. The problem is this!" He pointed to the image on Oracle. It showed a scene from the movie that had premiered the night before based on Morgan and Megan's story. On the paused frame was the actress seemingly portraying Morgan, she was tall and had somewhat darker hair with blood red highlights. The outfit she was wearing was fairly similar to the outfit Morgan had died in, though shorter than she would have ever been comfortable wearing, and her figure was a bit more generous than Morgan's own. She was draping herself over an older man in what seemed to be a bar, flirting for a drink perhaps with her arm around his neck.

"What the heck is this? Is that supposed to be me?"

"It is you, or rather it will be." Forseti quickly explained the release of the movie and the critical reception, as well as the plans to re-air it in the following days. "The problem becomes that by people believing that's you, then that's you. Hazard of being a goddess. Since your death you've been thought of as a victim, a sweet girl that made a mistake. Now, at least according to one critic, you're 'a bimbo archetype poured into skintight leather that she can't wait to get out of when anyone pays her attention.'"

"What the fuck? I mean sure I scammed a few dudes for drinks, but that's not me!"

"I know. It doesn't portray me much better. The film really paints it that you made a deal with me to get fame and hit it big, but I came to collect earlier than you expected. Most responses and comments I've seen have been something like 'don't play games with pagan gods, and don't be a whore.' Those were mostly older women, but there's an awful lot of them and people are listening. I think we're in trouble."

"Why? Energy is energy right? Good or bad, we survive, right?"

"Yeah, but what will we become? How long until this vocal group of grandmas influence those in power to limit our reach? There were brands starting to use my name and image, there were charities starting in your name to support various mental health and arts causes. Will anyone tie themselves to our names if this is who we are? Do you want to be that person?"

"Now that I know what it is I can control myself."

"Morgan, did you alter that dress after Frigg gave it to you?"

"No, it was shorter this morning. I actually think it's shorter now than it was when I put it on."

"You can't control it, the universe itself will bend you to your role."

"Well then," Morgan said after a deep breath, "perhaps we can control the narrative. Get out of the way."

"What are you going to do?" Forseti asked.

"I'm going to watch this movie, and then hit the forums to spin it. I'm fine with being a confident boss bitch, but I'm going to do it on my terms. You're going to figure out who made the movie and rain down some Viking wrath."

"Already a step ahead of you." Forseti pulled another video up of an interview on a talk show. The guest being interviewed looked a bit older and shorter, but it was undeniably Loki talking about making the movie.

"This guy again?!" Morgan wailed. "What more can you do than the things you've already done to him? What's worse than being tied to a boulder and having acid leaked on to you for years?"

"Being lawyered," Forseti said simply and made his way to his own chambers.

Morgan looked back to the movie clip. She checked her mom's social media. *This isn't who my Morgan was. She was brilliant and kind and was going to school to be an audio / video engineer. Don't remember her this way.* The comments section was turned off, though by the number of likes and other reactions it seemed the quote had been seen by quite a few. She let a tear fall into the surface of the basin.

21

Forseti sat down at his desk and summoned sheafs of parchment. He began by laying out everything he knew and had been told by others, which he hung in a timeline along a wall of his sitting room. Using a red thread to connect them all, he then wrote the open questions he had and hung them in their respective places as well as any assumptions he had come to. The events spanned from the Christianization of Norse territory until Forseti awoke recently, with most of the activity grouped at the ends and empty space in the middle.

The answer is somewhere in that gap. During that gap all of the gods slept, except Mimir and Loki. Loki isn't likely to tell me anything, and I've already spoken with Mimir. Mimir rarely is far from Odin's side, so talking to him may not be possible anyway. What was Loki doing for those centuries? He was supposed to be keeping our memory, preparing to cause our return. If so, how did he sustain himself unless he had followers? How could he have followers without feeding the rest of us, or at least some of us, energy? There's no Loki stories without the Aesir.

He decided the best course of action would be to learn as much as possible about the events he was aware of first and see what threads he may be able to pull from those. He summoned a Bible and began to research the upstart religion that had cost them so many losses and, ultimately, their relevance. Curling up into his favorite reading chair with a cup of tea, he settled in and began to read.

Morgan was furiously working her social media profiles, subtly and occasionally not so subtly working against the narrative the movie had created. She refused to be remembered as a goth bimbo, but after watching the movie she realized how much it had also portrayed Megan, her caring and compassionate friend, as a manipulator and kink enthusiast. *Although those knots they had her tie me in were pretty impressive... Wait, stop the hoe thoughts, those aren't you.* Even if it was too late for Morgan, Megan was still alive, and her trial was starting soon. This kind of publicity wouldn't help her. She was currently commenting on videos that had been posted this morning asking the US Presidential race nominees their thoughts on the movie, since anything Forseti seemed to be a political issue these days.

"I say again," said the well-dressed Thomas Cohen, "the story and the movie both shine a need for better crisis management, mental healthcare, and early warning systems for risky behaviors in our public schools. This was 2 recently graduated girls trying to make it in a world they weren't prepared for. I think the movie took some liberties with the girls' character, but that message was as clear to me as the day I first heard this terrible story."

"Liberties is an understatement!" Morgan's anonymous comment started. "I went to school with these girls, and they were nothing like portrayed. Megan was a quiet girl that was always willing to help others in classes and I saw her share her lunch with other kids a few times. Morgan was a bit louder, certainly not one to be bullied, but also kind. There's enough tragedy in this story without trying to sex it up or go for cheap entertainment."

The next video was a clip of his opponent, Todd Ridgway, calling into a conservative morning news program. "Well, it's terrible, you see, how far this country has fallen. You can see it in the movie, at least I'm told. Haven't seen it myself, but my wonderful advisors filled me in. These girls had their heads filled with mainstream media's praise of these sick social media sites and it's a shame. No prayer in schools, not even forced to stand to pledge the flag, such a shame. Mr. Laufison, who made the movie, is a great friend of mine and a tremendous producer. Did some deals with him in the day, he knows his stuff. I can tell you that we're going to change this, none of these false idols and social media are corrupting our kids when I'm re-elected." The clip continued to drone on as the hosts all bobbed their heads in agreement.

"I think the girls made a mistake," Morgan's puppet account that had been integrating itself into the comment section of the network's videos for weeks said. "The parents and teachers can only do so much against the media, I agree, but in this case I feel like the girls were filming what they thought would be a harmless video before they went to get burrito bowls. We've all heard the 911 tapes and the audio from the videos didn't sound like someone who intended to hurt anyone to me."

Thomas Cohen rode in his tour bus from a town hall on his way to a Presidential debate set for the next day. As the bus passed yet another corn field his staff milled around the kitchen area making coffee and decompressing. The meet and greet had gone well, a few hecklers, but Thomas was getting quite strong at giving them space to air their concerns and then redirecting them back to a solution that fit into his plan. He was making good inroads with the rural voters along with enjoying some top-quality BBQ. Despite the positives, he found himself staring out the window and getting hung up on an interaction he had with a constituent.

"You know," he said to his assistant, Kelly. "Last week, a gentleman made a passing comment referring to Democrats as idolators amid a tirade about prayer in schools. I shrugged that off as something being spread by right-wing pundits. Now, tonight, a young lady asserted that I was aligned with pagan gods and looking to bring about massive structural changes to the judicial system."

"Oh, that lady," Kelly grumbled with a slight sneer.

"Simply misinformed," Thomas interjected, "which I chocked up to another internet talking point. Though, now that I'm reflecting, I've been seeing more references to this Norse myth stuff. You handle my social media, has there been conversation out there associating our campaign with all this?"

"Ummm... Yeah, actually. Some of which we've leaned into, but only after some successful trends on Kuhlr."

"Walk me through this, how does a site where people share dance videos to old songs have anything to do with me? Are they doing that thing where they use my face with their lips to sing a song?"

"Nooo..." Kelly dragged out the word while she tried to figure out how to explain the ever-evolving world of social media to her boss. "See, when you want information about something you use a web search, right? The younger generation goes to Kuhlr and other social media sites. I see I'm losing you but hold on. If I want to know what the latest news is on a celebrity, a sports team, or a major event, I can either go to a news site and get the info that has been filtered and vetted through an agent or editor. Or I can search the term on Kuhlr and see videos from someone that was there and filming at the moment, or the athlete right after the game, or whatever."

She showed Thomas her phone and searched his name and the town they were just in. Videos of him talking to small groups of voters and eating a sandwich came up along with a few selfies with Mr. Cohen giving a thumbs up. "Stop doing the thumbs up, it's becoming a whole meme. Anyway, young voters, who we've established are the most impressionable and passionate demographic, aren't looking at press releases. They're searching Kuhlr and seeing what their peers are saying. So, your supporters are making videos drawing correlations between you and other relevant things. A particularly popular theme has been explaining your criminal reform policies and messaging about fighting corruption in politics through the lens of an already much discussed icon of fairness and judgement—Forseti. In fact, thanks to some of the videos created by our team, if you even search for Forseti on the app you'd have to scroll down a few pages before you see something related to the murder case. I'm not sure how it got onto the boomer radar, but I assume it's a convoluted misunderstanding of something bored housewives saw while death scrolling."

"That's... brilliant," Thomas conceded. "I didn't know we had a social media team though. I thought it was just you."

"Officially, yeah. I run your accounts. I connected with some other users on various sites that were spreading the same messages already and we bounced ideas off each other."

"Nice. What would I do without you?"

"Continue to eat bland pulled pork and drink terrible local beers in an effort to convert salty retirees by using logic to change their position from one that they didn't use logic to get into." Kelly said in a deadpan tone in what Thomas felt seemed like a rehearsed cadence.

"Since when did you become so jaded?"

"I'm always jaded, you're just now paying attention."

"I'm going to go back to staring out the window."

"You know?" Kelly added helpfully. "We did do one video of Forseti's face with your lips giving your 'No one is above the law' schtick."

෨ ෨ ෨

"Forseti," Odin acknowledged as his grandson walked into the hall.

"Allfather. I have a delivery for you," Forseti said without preamble as he handed him a parchment.

"What is this?" Odin muttered as he quickly scanned the document. "Is this a summons? You summon me to trial here, while I am holding a lecture?"

Forseti turned and looked at the rest of the room for the first time. Instead of the other Aesir seated in their thrones as he was used to, there were instead citizens and servants seated on the floor watching the exchange. "Oh, sorry, I didn't realize..."

"You didn't realize as you walked through a bunch of people to approach me, who was clearly speaking, that I was talking to those people?"

"I was a bit focused. Anyway, you've been served so I'll just... be on my way."

Odin set the parchment aside and continued his lecture.

～ ～ ～

President Ridgeway was flying from his latest rally to do one last speech before the debate. The press and his staff were gathered at the bar, while he was sipping a soda and talking with his advisor, Cindy. "How was the crowd, Cin? There had to be a thousand people!"

"Ticket sales indicate about 350." Cindy said tentatively.

"That many people snuck in for free? We need to increase security!"

"That reminds me," Cindy added with a bit of a wince, "the security company at the next venue said they weren't going to work unless we pay ahead. I guess they're owned by the same company that's..."

"Those scammers! One post and I'll have armed guards there, hold on. Where's my phone? The police love me, the citizens love me, I don't know what we worry about, let the people in, I always say."

"What about the ticket sales?" Cindy asked, confused.

"Well, they need to buy tickets. And merch, beautiful merch."

"Sir, we should prepare for the next speech. We missed the talking points on tax changes and trade agreements."

"I got carried away, but you're right. Hit the points, how can we work that into the speech we just did? I feel like I was on a good roll."

"You were sir. Here's what I was thinking," Cindy continued.

～ ～ ～

"What is the meaning of this?" Odin demanded walking into Forseti's hall, accompanied by other gods that had been summoned to court.

"Odin." Forseti acknowledged. "Apologies, but I'm in the middle of a lecture."

Odin looked around for a moment before spotting Morgan seated in a chair nearby. "Lecture? The only person here is your servant girl."

"I have no servants, this is Morgan and she is an Officer of the Court."

"Officer of the... Forseti what is this nonsense of a trial? Are you so bored? Are you holding a grudge for the Forgotten thing?"

"I assure you that judgement holds no grudges. Justice, however, demands pursuit until a judgement is rendered."

"Call off this Völva-hunt. I was within my rights as Allfather to take the actions I took to protect our way of life."

"I won't hear your case until the trial. Your premise, however, is flawed. You have been called as a witness, not as a defendant."

"Then who is..."

"What the Helheim is this?!" a voice erupted from the entrance as Loki marched into the hall. "The Court of Asgard V. Loki? What kind of Giant-hating puppet trial are you trying to pull off here Aesir?"

Forseti sighed, "Again, the trial begins tomorrow, and we will argue the merits of the case then."

"On what charges?" Loki scoffed.

"Attempted coup of the Norse pantheon." Forseti stated simply. "We'll discuss it tomorrow."

"I refuse to entertain this charade." Loki waved his hands dismissively and began to leave. As he grew closer to the door a stiff wind began to pick up, and Loki found himself struggling against it. Glancing back Loki realized that the clothes on the others in the hall weren't so much as blowing in a breeze and he slumped his shoulders to walk back to the gathering.

"I will see you all at midday tomorrow," Forseti announced as he rose from his seat. "Come, Morgan, we'll continue our lesson in my office."

23

"Good evening, America," a tall man said into the camera. "I'm Walt Isaacson, and welcome to the third and final Presidential Debate. We are one week from election day and our candidates are ready to make their cases for your votes." The dim stage behind him lit up in reds and blues as the candidates made their ways from opposite sides of the stage. They stopped to shake hands before going to their individual podiums. "Introducing the candidates, to my left is Democratic Party candidate Thomas Cohen, and to my right is President Todd Ridgeway, the Republican candidate."

After allowing sufficient time for applause from the live audience the host continued, "First, we will cover the rules of this debate. Each candidate will have a chance to answer the question, after which their opponent will be given time for a rebuttal. For this debate we've established a new restriction in which the opposition's microphone will be muted during the questioned candidate's answer. During rebuttal the microphones will be unmuted for both to allow a discussion." The TV broadcast ran a banner at the bottom of the screen informing the audience that the policy was agreed to by both candidates after a heated second debate where the host struggled to get the questions and answers on track. "We'll begin with opening remarks from candidate Cohen."

"Thanks, Walt. I'm glad to be here tonight and speak directly to the American people about the issues I care deeply about, as well as the issues they care about. While I've been traveling our great country I've had the opportunity to speak to thousands of hard working people that want to know how I plan to protect their safety, their finances, and their liberty. I hope to continue that conversation here with all those that I've not had the opportunity to speak with yet or that may not be inclined to come to one of my events."

"Thank you, Mr. Cohen. Now we'll hear opening remarks from President Ridgeway."

"Ladies and gentlemen in the audience, and at home all across this great country, I'm happy to be here. Let's be honest, there's work to do to continue to make this country, this amazing country, into an even greater nation and world power. My opponent talks about safety while freeing criminals and protecting money while funding socialist programs. For those that can see that's a smoke screen, I'm hoping to show you tonight that there's one path to fixing this country, and it's by reelecting me and maintaining control of congress so we can finish our work."

"Thank you, Mr. President. We'll pause here for a commercial break and have our first questions after this."

﹏ ﹏ ﹏

"Thank you all for coming." Forseti said as he took his seat on his throne in the main hall of Glitnir. The room had been rearranged to fit the needs of the trial with his seat at the rear wall of the room, another seat to his left for a witness stand and tables set up for the opposing sides. There was a large gallery with seats on either side of the room. The assembled gods sat orderly in the seats behind Loki's table with a few citizens seated in the rows across the aisle. "We are here to review the evidence that the Giant Loki sought to destroy the Asgardian realm through deception and direct action amongst the Midgardians. This hearing will be slightly different than we've done in the past as I've become more educated on Midgardian court practices and would like to adopt some of those. We will first hear the evidence and accounts from witnesses. After the prosecution has finished their case the defendant, Loki, will be given time to rebut the charges. As before I will render judgement based on the evidence presented and my decision will be final. As I cannot both prosecute and pass judgement, at least not since the 'Thor dressing up as Freyja and killing a bunch of Giants' trial..."

"8 years you made me work as a handmaiden!" Thor stood up and interrupted.

"And you looked so lovely while you did it," Freyja teased.

"In any case," Forseti continued, "the prosecution on behalf of Asgard will be done by Lady Morgan, who filed the charges." The court looked at the pale woman who was in a well-tailored dark blue dress with a matching jacket that Frigg had made for her. As a murmur began to build over the idea that a Midgardian sacrificial servant would be questioning one of their own Forseti hammered a gavel on his chair's arm. "Quiet! Morgan is no servant of mine nor anyone else. I have released her from service and while I am bound to ensure her existence per Odin's judgement, she has become an eternal in her own right through her own legend. Odin, Allfather and wisest of Aesir, look upon her and tell the audience what you see."

Odin looked at Morgan who met his gaze steadily. He looked deeper, seeing the connection she had to this realm. He could see her connection to Forseti, but she was not taking power from him, instead... "She has a spark of eternity. Energy flows to her from other realms and she owes nothing to Forseti." Odin continued to look at Morgan as she turned back to the trial. He had, of course, seen other mortals gain fame enough to exist on their own before. Ragnar Lothbrok, Eric Bloodaxe, and a few others. They had fought great battles and were celebrated in remembrance by their armies, though. This girl was sacrificed, and her spark burned brighter than some of the gods he currently sat among.

"Now, that's settled. We'll begin with opening arguments. Morgan, please state your purpose."

"The case I will present will show, beyond a doubt, that the Giant Loki manipulated his fellow gods to plot the collapse of the Asgardian pantheon. Through his direct actions while you slept, he nearly succeeded, and only through his own hubris did he fail. His oversight of a small shrine in Canada and the unfortunate fall of a slippery knife have led us here. Through careful research and collaboration, I was able to untangle the web that was spun and I look forward to illustrating his misdeeds to you." Morgan straightened her lapels, turned to Forseti and winked before taking a seat. *Nailed it. I'm no lawyer, but I've watched enough serial dramas to know how to build suspense.*

"Now the court will ask the defendant for opening remarks."

"My friends, this is Bull Skitr. Forseti is still upset about the prank on Balder and that he wasn't as memorable as the rest of you. I've not done anything that didn't serve the greater mission of preserving our people and avoiding Ragnarok. I have worked tirelessly for you, my Aesir and Vanir family, to protect you from the increasingly dangerous world out there, where fewer believe in gods than ever before and their so-called science is able to explain how the natural world works, leaving us without purpose. I've done nothing more than trying to make Asgard great again."

As Loki took his seat Forseti instructed Morgan to call her first witness. When Morgan called on Odin to testify there was a collective gasp among the gallery. Odin rose and walked towards the seat to Forseti's left. As he approached the marble floor of Glitnir shaped itself around the wooden seat that had been there, creating a large gleaming throne of silver and gold.

"Before you are seated," Morgan began quietly, almost as if the words were choked out before regaining the strength of her voice, "Mr. Allfather, we ask that you take an oath of true-intention." This was a gamble, possibly a deadly one, but one she and Forseti had prepared for and agreed was necessary.

"You think me a liar, small human? I am many things, but a liar is not one of them. I've nothing to hide nor do I fear the consequences of my actions."

"Then we should be able to agree to a simple and narrowly focused oath." Morgan kept her eyes trained on Odin. She wanted to glance towards Forseti for reassurance or for him to interject and insist on it as a rule of the court, but she knew that this part was on her. They had to get Odin to agree to an oath. If he took it anyone else at the stand would have no choice but to follow his example. If he refused though... "It is standard procedure in modern trials."

"Perhaps. What would you have me agree to?" Odin asked guardedly.

"That anything you say while in this court is true to the best of your knowledge. That you'll answer all questions from myself, Forseti, and Loki to the best of your ability and without any withholding of information that is relevant to give a full account. That you will not offer any other commentary except to answer the questions you are asked by myself or Loki during our turns to question or Forseti at any time. Your oath will be satisfied upon being dismissed from your testimony by Forseti." Morgan checked her notes to make sure she hadn't missed anything. This part was critical, as the Norse had held oaths and vows to be the most significant ties one could make to another.

Indeed, Loki owed much of his not being dead at the hands of the Aesir he had wronged to an oath Odin had made long ago to him. While the vows were taken seriously, that didn't stop the gods from looking for holes in the oath to take advantage of.

"Will you agree to those terms?"

"Yes, of course. Those terms are fine," Odin agreed before reciting them back as his assent. Afterwards, he sat quietly in his chair and waited for Morgan to ask her first question. Morgan sighed internally with relief, her first gambit had succeeded.

"Mr... do you have a surname?"

"Burrson," Odin responded

"Really? Should I call you Mr. Burrson?"

"No."

"How should I address you formally?"

"Allfather will do. Though I have always liked Hrafnagud, or Fjolnir..."

"Odin will be fine, Morgan," Forseti interrupted. Knowing his grandfather had been called by hundreds of names he wanted to cut off the train of thought lest the "all relevant" clause inspired Odin to go off the rails.

"Right." Morgan got herself refocused. "Can you tell the court, Odin, what your intention was by having Loki act on Earth to cause the Forgetting?" She decided she was claiming *the Forgetting* as her term, as she hadn't heard a better name for it and it was catchy.

"Objection," Loki's voice interrupted. "Speculation."

"Are you saying that Odin would only be speculating on his own intentions?" Forseti asked.

"No, she's speculating on Odin's intentions in sending me to Midgard!"

"It's hardly speculation when he confirmed it in a public audience."

"Then objection, prejudicial questioning."

"No," Forseti said simply. At seeing Loki's insulted look, he continued. "This isn't an American court. I'll hear your objections, but I'll rule on them only if they serve the truth. There are no legal loopholes here, only truth. Go ahead and answer Allfather."

"Sure," Odin began. "My intention was to avoid Ragnarok."

"How would this plan have worked, exactly?" Morgan probed.

"By taking advantage of the noise being caused by the Christian upstarts. With their surge and the Norse spreading into the new world I foresaw a similar fate to what became of the eastern pantheons. The Greeks, the Romans, and others had become weaker, but continued to exist through their legacy. I learned much of their story through Mimir's well, as I also learned that Ragnarok is a cycle. The last time it happened, as has happened every time, the Allfather of that age built on the work of the ages before him to prevent the cycle from repeating. He came closer than ever before, because he realized that trying to put out the fires and prevent the prophecy was a fool's errand.

"Instead, he worked to hide the prophecy, rationalizing that the gods of the time wouldn't know how to prevent anything. While it ultimately failed, his decision to send someone to Midgard to suppress information fascinated me. I realized that his vision had been too narrow in this. Why merely suppress information when you could create a new story? I've known since I drank from Mimisbrunnr that it didn't really matter what we did here, it mattered what the Midgardians, the humans, believed.

"My plan became desperate when Balder was killed, but I had decided that having the humans forget about Ragnarok, forget about us nearly completely, would reduce the threat. I hid how dependent we are on the beliefs of Midgard from the other gods so that they wouldn't interfere, and I sent Loki to conceal our existence until such a time we could be brought back with a new story. A story without Ragnarok, a story without the prophecy that leads to Ragnarok."

"A story without some of your fellow gods?" Morgan interrupted.

"In some cases, yes. If those gods were so tied to the events that would cause the conflict that results in destruction, I felt it safer to sacrifice them for the greater good."

"When did you speak to Loki about this plan?"

"While he was restrained in the cave."

"Why did you approach him with this?"

"He has proven to be capable of influencing many. He is also central to the events of Ragnarok. His children would lead the force that destroyed all and as the events began to unfold, I could see how our treatment of him, our punishments, would lead to their revolt. I wanted to offer a truce and he was the most capable agent I could think of for my purposes."

"What was Loki's price? Did he agree to help for only his freedom?"

"No. He wanted the freedom to operate as he needed, his freedom from bondage, and Forseti to be removed from our story. He resented Forseti for his punishments."

"And you agreed to these terms?" Morgan asked

"Yes." Odin said flatly. "If it came to losing one Aesir in the name of vengeance or losing the world when Loki's children sought vengeance, it wasn't really a choice."

"How much of the final plan did Loki influence?"

"Very little. I planned and spoke with Mimir to strengthen the plan and conveyed it to Loki. He made suggestions based on his history with the humans and proposed ways to rebuild our legacy. It was his idea to integrate our story into religions so that they would be easier to accept and understand when the time was right."

"Did he indicate to you that all the other gods would sleep while he acted on Earth?"

"Yes. I was aware that we would need to slumber while our story was changed and retold."

"Did he indicate how he would stay awake and able to work while everyone else was forgotten?"

"He said that if he was able to gain supporters in his human form, he would be empowered by them without a need for his story to be told as he would be living a new story."

"Thank you for your time, Allfather." Morgan returned to her table while

Loki stood to cross examine Odin. "Just, one more question if I may," she interjected before sitting down, causing Loki to awkwardly hover over his seat and look to Forseti.

"Go ahead, but please ensure you're prepared to end your questioning next time," Forseti admonished.

"Sorry, slipped my mind," Morgan said, just as she had rehearsed the previous day. "Odin, if you had known that Loki's plan included establishing himself in another pantheon and allowing the Norse gods to remain asleep, would you have sent him on this mission?"

"Well... of course not," Odin stuttered, taken aback at the implication that had just been made. He looked towards Loki, who was midway between sitting and standing and looking rather bewildered. "That wasn't the plan we had discussed at all."

"Thank you, I'm done with my questioning now." She turned to Loki and locked eyes with him, a smirk on her lips. "Your witness."

༄ ༄ ༄

"Our next question comes from our livestream," Walt Isaacson tells the candidates. "How do you plan to deliver on your campaign promises in an increasingly divided establishment? Mr. President, we'll start with you."

"Thanks, Walt, and thank you viewer for your great question. As you know we campaigned making big promises before our last election to rid D.C. of corruption, reduce the tax burden on the working men and women, and secure our borders from foreign criminals. In the past four years we launched dozens of investigations into former government officials and through a strong relationship with Congress was able to pass laws making tougher punishments for traitors and those careless with classified documents. We passed the biggest tax break on middle America in history while still growing our military and border security. We've been able to do amazing things these last few years and look forward to kicking those efforts into overdrive during my next term as we continue to strengthen our position on the world stage."

"Thank you, Mr. President. Mr. Cohen, your rebuttal and answer?"

"Great question from the viewer at home, Walt, but I'm afraid the President didn't answer it any more than he has any direct questions tonight. If we look at his original campaign promises against his supposed successes we can see that the goal posts have been moved constantly throughout his first term. The only corruption that has been exposed has been in his own staff. The congressional investigations have cost the taxpayers millions and have resulted in no charges. The tax cut that has been much discussed has a poison pill that very clearly shows a massive increase in a couple years for most Americans and another cut for the richest in the form of more loopholes and exemptions for items only those people can afford. You can't shoot a hole in a barn wall and then go draw the target around it and claim a bullseye. You also can't ram legislation through on just the strength of party control that the average American doesn't agree with, then beg for another term to work on the things that matter to them. My administration will work with both parties to determine a path forward that works for our country and building on the things that have been proven to work in other countries around the world. If we're unable to build consensus with our colleagues across the aisle we will work as hard as we have during this campaign to educate and discuss with you, the voters, what we want to accomplish and why we may be getting stopped from doing so. The voters will decide who is acting in their interests and if the people that have the privilege to serve them are working against them, we will work tirelessly to provide a candidate that will serve them."

24

"For our next topic we'll start with Mr. Cohen. Campaign finance reform and accountability has been a hot topic inside the beltway for years, and you've talked on it extensively in ads and town halls. How do you respond to accusations from your challenger and Political Action Committees that your campaign has contracted social media influencers off the books?"

"I'm glad you asked," Thomas Cohen began. "While we haven't felt the need to address these silly speculations and would rather focus on our policies, there has been enough noise made by my opponent that casual observers may think there's something to it. I want to be clear, we do not pay social media personalities to promote us. While some may be paid by PACs, the majority of posts are simply young Americans that are drawn to our cause and understand that another four years of regressive policies will only damage their future. I also want to state that our campaign has kept immaculate records and been very careful in the way we use our funding to set the example of how we think campaign funds should be used. While we are still waiting to see my opponent's records from their campaign last election, where there are questions about an over two-million-dollar discrepancy, we are prepared to submit our financials for audit immediately."

"Thank you." Walt Isaacson continued, shifting his view towards the other candidate. "President Ridgway, your response?"

"You know, these accusations are getting old," the President began. "We've said, time and again, that those records are subject to an audit and we won't be releasing them until the proper authorities have finished their review, as any responsible businessperson would tell you. Offering to just throw around your financials to prove a point doesn't make you a good deal maker, it makes you an easy target. It goes to show you how inexperienced my tax and spend opponent is. Unprepared for the world stage."

"Ms. Green," Forseti began after their break, "call your next witness, please."

"I would like to call Mimir." Morgan announced.

"Oh, present!" Mimir called out. The court looked around a bit before a few moved aside and Mimir was visible, a head sitting on a chair beside Odin. "I may require some assistance." Odin lifted Mimir and walked him to the witness stand, which formed itself to a pedestal to accommodate him.

"Mimir," Morgan said, "Would you please reiterate the same oath as Odin took? Do you need me to say it again for you."

"No, darling. I've quite a good memory." Mimir recited the oath of truth and looked expectantly at Morgan.

"Mimir... can I call you Mim?"

"Of course, I prefer it, actually," Mimir said with a smile. Morgan smiled and nodded to him. Forseti had told her Mim would be a kind witness, but ingratiating herself with a comfortable nickname and connection would help things along.

"Mim, you were awake during the entire time that the other gods slept?"

"I was. Turns out being nothing more than a head covered in embalming spices doesn't require much energy."

"Do you recall the conversations between Odin and Loki as they were planning their actions?"

"I do."

"Was Odin's account accurate to what you remember?"

"It is an accurate account of what was discussed and planned."

"As the only other witness to what transpired during the long slumber, would you say that the plan was executed as laid out?"

"Objection!" Loki interjected. "Foundation issues, we can't assume Mimir was able to observe what happened during that time."

"Upheld." Forseti agreed. "Morgan, redirect."

"Mim, were you able to monitor events on Earth during this time?"

"Not in the sense that Heimdall sees the other realms, or how Forseti can see through his pedestal. Through my connection to Yggdrasil, gained by living in its roots and drinking of its well for many years, I am able to sense what is going on in the nine realms. I am able to know it as a memory and as surely as if I had seen it myself."

"Objection." Loki stood again. "Speculation. We can't prove that Mimir doesn't have that ability, but it does mean he wasn't a direct witness to the events he claims to have knowledge of. He may know the results, but not the intention or actions that lead to them."

"It's a good point, Loki. Give me a moment to confer with the smartest being to ever live to determine the path forward." Forseti turned to Mimir's pedestal. "Do you think you are a credible witness and able to give accurate testimony?"

"Yes."

"Great, please continue." Forseti turned back towards Loki who slumped in his seat a bit.

"So," Megan resumed without missing a beat, "would you say that the plan was executed the way it was discussed in the meetings you witnessed?"

"I wouldn't." Mimir began. "It began without issue. Loki worked to gather writings and artifacts which he stored away as Christianity continued to spread into the northern territories. He quietly influenced Leif Erikson to convert, who then spread the new religion to the upstart settlements in Vinland and Greenland. With Europe well converted and the western expansion cut off, the time of our followers was over within a Midgardian generation. The next phase though, is where the differences came. The original plan was to distribute relics after a period of time to be "discovered" and to gain excitement in the historian circles. Loki was also to work against the Christians, to build distrust among the population and build a core of followers to revive the old ways. Unfortunately, it was a flawed premise."

"What do you mean?"

"Religion and myths are ephemeral. In our time, as people spread and encountered other people their beliefs would merge and become something new. We expected the cycle to continue. As Christianity began to falter we would make a resurgence with our original texts. We assumed the migration period would end and humanity would settle into its individual areas, where we would be able to convert a population back that would be able to sustain us again, albeit at a lesser quantity."

"So, they were planning to leave some gods forgotten?"

"Yes. Forseti would have been the highest of those left behind, but many lesser Aesir, Vanir, and Giants were eliminated from the texts as well."

"What happened that things went astray?"

"Midgard advanced in ways we weren't expecting. First with means of travel, then influence of art, and eventually their technology and communication abilities. Christianity, along with its brother religions known as the Abrahamic religions, didn't burn out. It came at a time that allowed it to be preserved and spread far beyond any that came before. With the travel and communications, it was able to continually reinforce itself far beyond its centers of influence in a way the Romans would have wept to see. Loki began to reintroduce our artifacts around three hundred years later and a scholar began to document our stories. It was slow to start, but Loki was able to take advantage of the growing media and around a hundred years ago the stories were able to sustain the first of the Aesir to reawaken. The timeline was much slower than we anticipated and in a way we couldn't have predicted, but it eventually worked out."

"So, working with the Christians was part of Loki's mission?" Morgan asked.

"It was. He was to give them information that would allow them to integrate the Norse more effectively. It allowed them to merge our holidays and some other parts of our history. Later, those similarities allowed the modern humans to relate to and appreciate the Norse stories."

"Thank you, Mim," Morgan said as she began to walk back to her seat. Loki stood and straightened his shirt. "Last question," Morgan said just before crossing behind her desk. "Would there have been any reason for Loki, who's now standing for some reason, to work with them before this plan began?"

"No..." Mimir said with a hint of confusion "Not that I can figure."

"Thank you, Mim," she said as she took her chair and looked expectantly at Loki. She knew doing it twice was pushing it, but she couldn't help herself.

"No questions," Loki stated, clearly off his game.

"Mimir, thank you for your testimony, you are released from your vow," Forseti said. As Odin came to collect the head Forseti announced another break as it was lunch. While the gods milled around the food at the back of the hall Morgan found him to discuss the case.

"Do the Valkyrie's usually hang around hearings? They like your bailiffs?" Morgan asked.

"Not normally. They're either here for their own entertainment or were told to be here." Forseti had noticed the arrival of a few of the warrior maidens midway through Mimir's testimony. "The only ones who could summon them are Odin and Freyja."

"Maybe they're just here for entertainment?" Morgan shrugged.

"Thrud, maybe. She enjoys a power battle. Mist and Kara, though, have never come to a hearing." He indicated towards the pair standing apart, one with wispy grey wings and the other with curly hair and wild eyes. Thrud, Morgan remembered, was Thor's daughter and she stood talking with him over a tray of smoked pork.

"What about the other one?" Morgan nodded towards the last Valkyrie that had shown up and still stood in the doorway observing the room.

"That's Sigrun. If she's here, I assume Freyja requested her and is expecting something to happen. The question is which side might find themselves at the end of her spear."

"Guess we better make a good case..." Morgan said as she walked towards the food.

"For my last witness," Morgan started, "I call Loki." A collective inhale rippled through the audience, giving Morgan an opportunity to gauge her audience. The seating had shifted subtly, with Odin and Frigg sitting on Morgan's side of the court along with Balder, Nanna, Frey, and Freyja. Loki's side of the court was thinning, but still contained Thor, Sif, Ran, and Hel. A few more Valkyrie had shown up and were scattered among the back rows of the chamber. Loki stood and made his way to the witness stand.

"One change to the oath," Forseti called before Morgan was able to begin. "While Loki must swear to tell the truth and be forthcoming in his testimony, when his answer may incriminate himself he cannot be compelled to answer. I understand this is a different procedure than we've used in the past, but is aligned with current lawspeaking process in Midgard." Loki swore his oath and sat.

"Mr. Laufison, is the testimony we've heard so far here today accurate to your recollection of the events?" Morgan asked.

"They are, but please, call me Loki."

"Mr. Laufison, would you also agree that Odin and Mim were complete in their recollection of the planning details?"

"Yes, I believe they were."

"Then why, Loki, did you fail to tell them that you had already delayed Ragnarok and were establishing yourself to overtake another pantheon?"

"I... objection!" Loki stuttered.

"Sustained. Morgan, redirect." Forseti looked to the audience and noticed the shift as everyone leaned forward just a bit. He had been unsure when Morgan's strategy had included accusations that would ultimately be stricken from the record, but trusted in her ability to build the drama and ultimately influence the outcome.

"Okay. Loki, did you ever inform the Allfather that you were already working to destroy the Norse pantheon when you brought this plan to him?"

"Morgan!" Forseti interrupted. "Establish your premise before casting these assertions."

"Fine." Morgan feigned annoyance and turned her back on the Giant and Aesir at the front of the court, staring over the heads of the audience for a moment and she took a breath and observed the postures of those seated in the gallery. "Mr. Laufison, have you read the Christian texts?"

"I have."

"Have you noticed the similarities in their stories and the history of the Norse gods?"

"Every religion has overlap, they influence each other and grow from older tales. Your previous witnesses pointed out this as a part of our strategy." Loki was regaining confidence and his tone became more relaxed.

"It is interesting, though, that their earliest texts, which predate the earliest Norse texts, have so many stories that reflect the Norse tales, even though these religions were separated by many miles and years. Would you agree?"

"I'm not able to..." Loki found himself unable to finish the sentence and stuttered.

"Let me help you." Morgan cut him off and walked closer. "What sentence were you about to say, understanding that you're answering this question and not the one that sentence would have answered?"

After some hesitation Loki stared into the middle distance and said, "I cannot answer that question without risking self-incrimination."

"Because you were going to say 'I'm not able to answer that.' when in fact you could answer that and your vow won't allow you to tell a lie. Is that the issue?"

"I cannot answer that question without risking self-incrimination." At this point there was an audible shuffle of postures in the gallery as gods became more focused on the trial and the Valkyries' wings began to flutter as if they were stretching.

"Loki," Morgan took a gentler tone as she could see her opponent's hesitation and nervousness, "did *you* have anything to do with those old Christian stories?"

"I cannot answer..."

"I know." Morgan cut him off. "How about admitting to the gods in front of you, or to the god of judgement sitting beside you, that you created the Abrahamic religions after the last Ragnarok cycle to ensure your survival when you ultimately collapsed the Norse pantheon?"

"Objection..."

"Withdrawn." Morgan raised her voice. "Perhaps you can just tell us the story of Genesis and the Garden of Eden? Adam and..."

"Parlay!" Loki shouted, looking to Forseti. "I'd like to parlay."

The audience was on their feet now and shouting towards the bench. Forseti banged his gavel trying to restore order before rolling his eyes and raising his arms silencing the hall. It took the assembled gods a moment to realize their screams were quieted and a few instead switched to hand gestures to make their points to the judge. They also found themselves unable to approach the proceedings. "Silence!" Forseti called. "There will be order. The Giant Loki has called for a parlay with his accuser, The Human Morgan. We will meet in my chambers, and I will mediate. You are welcome to stay and have refreshments, but as long as you are in the walls of Glitnir you will be unable to raise your voices above conversation and my chambers will remain soundproofed from the rest of the hall."

25

"Ladies and gentlemen of our audience both here and watching from home," Walt Isaacson smiled into the camera, "welcome back to this final debate between our leading Presidential candidates. Many questions have been answered and we're to the part of the night where our candidates will make their final pleas to the voters before they head to the polls next week. We'll start with Democratic candidate Thomas Cohen."

"Thank you, Walt," Mr. Cohen began. "I want to reiterate that our campaign is committed to delivering a Presidency that represents *all* Americans. We believe that America cannot move forward, or reclaim a position of greatness, without improving the lives of all our people. Don't let my opponent rewrite history. How many more militias must he activate to protest local elections? How many more people will he give access to our greatest intelligence who go on to be arrested for corruption? I ask you to consider what this country stands for when you cast your vote, and I'll finish by promising that when I cast my vote, I will be thinking only of how I can serve America, not how it can serve me."

"Thank you, Mr. Cohen. President Ridgway, your closing statements?"

༄ ༄ ༄

Less than an hour had passed in Forseti's office, and the parties were finalizing their agreement. Loki stared across the round table at Forseti. "You don't intend to punish me?"

"If you hold up your end of the deal, the anger of your fellow gods will be punishment enough." Forseti assured him.

"Well, I've certainly endured that before. Fine. You have a deal." Loki shook hands with Forseti and Morgan before they moved to the door. "Wait. Before we go, I want to say 'well done' to your apprentice. I have no doubt much of this was orchestrated, but you aren't clever enough to trick me on your own, Forseti. Well done, Morgan. I look forward to seeing what you do in your time among us."

"Thanks." Morgan smiled. "If you do your part that'll be a long time, too."

Once back in the hall of Glitnir the three were greeted by a full gallery of observers. It appeared that nearly every god and Valkyrie had assembled, and the hall had added seating for them all, who were mostly on the side that had been Morgan's. Forseti took his seat on the dais, with Loki and Morgan standing to the side. "Aesir, Vanir, Giants, and all other friends assembled. Loki has agreed to give an account of his actions to settle the investigation and will accept my judgement. He is still bound by his oath but will swear to modify it to force the truth, even if it would be injurious to himself. To ensure Morgan's accusations are satisfied she will continue questioning in order to clarify her case. Loki, do you accept the new oath and the terms I've set forth?"

"I do." Loki said and took his seat on the stand again, looking to the floor. Forseti nodded to Morgan to continue.

"Loki, were you present during the events of the last Ragnarok?"

"I was." A muffled gasp came from the crowd that Forseti had decided to leave under volume control for expediency. "I survived the cycle by shapeshifting to a human, called Lif, and hid with the gods and human woman that survived the cycle. The end was rather well prophesied so as the events drew nearer, I followed the Modi of that cycle to their hiding spot and killed the real Lif."

"I thought the Allfather of the last cycle hid the prophecies?" Morgan clarified.

"He did." Loki nodded. "Though not all that well. As Ragnarok began, he realized that there was no use hiding it anymore, allowing my army to acquire some of the info. I had another shape shifter take my appearance and roll while I hid. My army thought I was trying to outsmart the prophecy by going to help Fenrir..."

"So, you survived Ragnarok, but wasn't Lif to begin a new cycle with his human woman companion? What happened next?"

"When we re-emerged into the remade world, I was unable to produce human offspring with my bride. What was to be our first born emerged as a goat, she died in labor."

"And how did the events after this lead to the world being repopulated, and your scheme to jump pantheons?" Morgan asked kindly, knowing she had won and not wanting to rub his nose into it too much.

"Later, the reborn Odin and his brothers would visit Midgard. They carved the first people from trees and left them on their own. Once they had left, I befriended Ash and Yew and showed them how to survive in nature, and how to become educated. They were little more than animals and I knew I would need help getting them to become the people that could repopulate the realm as I had failed. I brought them an apple from the garden of Idunn, which they ate. They lived longer, became wise quickly, and went on to birth children and raise a small village. They knew nothing of the gods that had made them and only remembered glimpsing one of them breathing life into them. I decided then to change the cycle.

"I told them of an unnamed god and even disguised myself as a grand form to occasionally guide them. I had always appeared to them as a talking serpent and continued to play both roles. I couldn't tell them my names. If Odin returned to the realm and they spoke of Loki I would be caught. If they spoke of Lif, the other gods would be alerted that something was off as well. I chose Lucifer. I've always been partial to L names."

There was silence in the hall while the gods tried to absorb what they had heard. Morgan let the news settle a moment before continuing, "And then what happened? You're here, something must have changed."

"Indeed." Loki looked up from the floor into her eyes, his face tired and regretful. "I didn't understand the nature of gods then. As their children grew and generations spread, their worship of 'God' gave an unexpected surprise— God showed up one day as if they had always been there. With that spot occupied, I was relegated to my other role as the serpent. Over the years, God began to distrust me, and I became a rival.

"By the time humans were able to write their beliefs down I had been framed as their Satan. A silver-tongued trickster that causes trouble was a role I was born for, so I played along for millennia. This is the time that the Germanic religion began to spread as well, and as it made its way to the north it evolved into what would become the Norse religion.

"Apparently, Odin and his brothers had been busy as well. My Satanic duties were quite simple, just existing as an unknowable tale of distrust and keeping a low profile, so I went to Jotunheim and became Loki once again. What better way to gain power than to absorb energy from two religions, right?"

Odin and the other gods were pacing the floor and glaring between Loki and Forseti, unsure which to aim their wrath at for being unable to intervene.

"It was fun, until God sent his kid to mess things up. That's when I found myself taking a more active role to prevent becoming obscure. When

Balder died and I went into hiding, I was in the desert with God's kid. It was becoming too much to do both and being chained to a huge fucking boulder with the entrails of my child while a snake dripped venom on me didn't give me a reason to stick with this group.

"When Odin approached with a peace offering, I saw my opportunity. I manipulated him into the plan, which I used as an opportunity to weaken this pantheon and spread the Christian religion, securing my place."

"Then something happened?" Morgan asked.

"The more the kid, Joshua, talked about Satan and how much of a danger I was, my power grew." Loki looked bitterly at the audience. "Then Satan showed up, and he was a lot more aggressive than me. No longer a fallen angel that liked to play pranks, he had been made into a vengeful demon that only sought the destruction of man. I was out of a home again, and I fled. I had saved most of what I had hidden from our stories and began placing them to be found. I traveled the land and told our stories, pretended to be a Lawspeaker and wrote the history as if it had been told to me by others. Slowly I was able to feel power flowing back into me as Loki became a recognized name again. I had time on my side and invested it wisely. Over the centuries my companies influenced the stories that would be told, and eventually the Norse stories were told enough that the gods began to wake again. I've been working to strengthen the pantheon ever since."

Forseti turned from Loki and looked towards the audience and his eyes widened. The assembled gods were pressing against the barrier that they could not cross. The Valkyries were positioned in the rafters and by the exit with their spears ready and Loki stared back at them defiantly.

"That's right," Loki said to them. "I tried to bury you all for my own gain and when it blew up in my face I came crawling back. But it's been me, no one else, that has gotten you back on your feet. I've been putting in the work and I'm sorry for what I did. Things got out of hand, but can you blame me for being tired of getting the pointy end of the prod? You didn't bat an eye when I had to give birth to a horse that Odin then stole for his own transport. Or when my other children were tortured or discarded for the power they may one day wield. Yeah, I was still the bad guy in their stories, but I was respected. Besides, I did what I was supposed to do, I stopped Ragnarok. The cycle is broken."

"I rest my case," Morgan said quietly.

"Then I will render judgement," Forseti said as he signaled the gods to be seated, which they did with wicked grins on their faces. They expected cruelty,

135

they hadn't learned that the world had changed yet. "It is my judgement that continuing the cycle of harsh treatment against Loki and his family that has led to our destruction for cycles unknown is unwise, especially in light of the new world we find ourselves in.

"Our lifeforce isn't tied to worshippers anymore, but to scholars and enthusiasts. None are able to harness this energy the way Loki has proven himself to, though he has been under the yoke of his own hatred in deciding what stories to tell. I hereby free you of that, Loki. I am sorry for the way we have all treated you in the past, and I hope that we can move forward to better our entire pantheon. It is my judgement that the Giant Loki will continue his work on Earth, but that he will work to tell all of our stories and reawaken any gods that still slumber. Through his efforts we will become more powerful than we have ever been, and we can find our way without the threat of Ragnarok over us. Does this please the petitioner?" Forseti looked expectantly to Morgan.

"It does." She nodded.

"Does this please the Allfather?" Forseti stood and turned towards Odin. He knew he needed his blessing for this to work. Forseti's judgement was binding, but without Odin's acknowledgement, there was nothing to keep the crowd from tearing Loki apart as soon as the barrier was removed.

Odin stared at Loki for a long moment. Odin was no fool, though he was enraged at having been tricked. He glanced to Mimir who raised an eyebrow, his version of a nod. He knew his answer would mean either an uneasy peace in the realms or the death of Loki.

If Loki died, would any be able to carry on his work and keep them alive? Would they be able to stand against the other pantheons who were more well versed with today's communication and had true believers?

"It pleases me," Odin said simply.

෴ ෴ ෴

"On the charge of Involuntary Manslaughter in the case of Megan Mays, how does the jury find?"

"We find the defendant not guilty, Your Honor."

There were words said that Megan didn't hear after that, she had collapsed into her seat and immediately began crying. The trial had been painful, having to relive that night every day while the media and prosecutors speculated on what she had been doing and why she had done it. Her defense had done a good job getting the jury to see her as a misguided and troubled young woman, one who had gotten caught up in the moment and lost track of the knife. It had been enough, at least one juror had decided she had suffered enough.

Lori Lochlan emerged from the courthouse via the rear exit with the rest of the jurors, away from the press. She walked up to the man and woman waiting at a nearby car and got in the backseat. The car pulled around and across the street from the courthouse where the man and woman stepped out of the vehicle, but this time with another man.

"I was really not popular in that jury room." Loki mumbled.

"But you got the job done, that's what matters." Forseti said. They watched Megan emerge from the courthouse to a crowd of camera shutters and news reporters crowding her. Megan avoided the cameras, flanked by police officers that helped her to the car her parents waited in nearby. Megan looked across the street and locked eyes with the woman standing by the car quietly watching. She hesitated, the tall redhead could have been a cardboard cutout of her friend. *Probably an actress for the next TV movie getting into character...*

Morgan watched her friend get into the car and pull away. Tears came down her cheek as she saw Megan glance back towards them through the rear window. "Thank you, Loki." she whispered.

"One more stop to go." Forseti said.

Ava was sitting in a coffee shop trying not to appear nervous. Her mother and father were with her sipping their drinks and watching the door anxiously. The agent had called and requested a meeting. Instead of pulling Ava from school they had agreed to meet in the shop that was near her father's university office. The tables were full of students working at their laptops on projects and a few had nodded to Dr. Tillmann when they had entered. A tall man walked in accompanied by a shorter bearded man and a red-haired woman. They made their way to the Tillmann's table and exchanged names and pleasantries.

"Ava, we're excited to meet you." The tall man, Logan, said with a smile. "We received a draft of your book from one of our publishing partners that thought we may be interested." Ava had been working to publish a book on Norse Mythology geared towards young adults. "We think exploring the Norse pantheon and making it engaging for a mass audience is a great opportunity. It has been popular with more adult Viking-style themes, but we think there's a lot of potential for a more family friendly approach."

"Y... You do?" Ava stuttered.

"We do. We would be proud to help you publish your book and join our team as the youngest author we've ever worked with. What do you say?"

"We would need to see the offer." Harrison Tillmann intervened.

"Of course, here we are." Logan produced a pair of contracts. "While my associates here are experts on Norse and other Germanic religions, we would also like to extend an offer to you, Dr. Tillmann, to serve as freelance historical consultant should Ava join us. We'd be happy to pay you a modest fee, of course."

"See, Loki?" Morgan said as they walked back towards their car. "Doesn't it feel better to help people than trying to get over on them?" She sipped on her latte enjoying the sensation and becoming determined to get an espresso machine into Asgard.

"It's all right, I suppose." Loki pondered. "We could have made them beg or at least haggle a bit instead of just giving them a generous contract."

"Not the point," Forseti pointed out. "The goal is to get the stories out. They are much more motivated to put out a quality product now. Sequels too."

"Can we go back and get a donut? I forgot I can't gain weight now and regret not getting donuts." Morgan turned and headed back to the café. Forseti and Loki watched after her.

"You sure about all this?" Loki asked.

"Nope," Forseti responded. "But I think we'll have a better shot at it working together."

Author's Notes

Thank you for taking the time to read my first attempt at a novel. I've learned a lot from the experience and figured I'd document some of the choices I made in the story as well share some general info on the characters and settings for anyone that may be interested.

What inspired the story?

I began writing this story in the spring of 2022 after seeing a writing prompt on Reddit along the lines of *'A child makes a sacrifice to a long-forgotten god and the god is reawakened to protect them'*. Why this prompt stuck with me, I don't know, but it made for good shower thoughts for a while and eventually I started looking for a candidate deity. I centered on Norse fairly quickly, knowing that little contemporary writings existed. In fact, the most common resources we have are *The Prose Edda* and *The Poetic Edda*. I reference these vaguely when Morgan is explaining things to Forseti. The Poetic Edda was written in the 13th century and lost until the mid-1600s and contains many of the tales used to inform this writing. If you're interested in digging further, I'd recommend Jackson Crawford's translation. (Side note— the guy in the cowboy hat from Colorado that Ava interviews is a shout out to Jackson Crawford. His YouTube and his books were huge influences, even if I did stray from the source material a bit). The Prose Edda was written by a Lawspeaker, Snorri Sturluson, and is closer to a textbook analyzing Norse myths, including those told in the Poetic Edda. The earliest writing comes from circa 1220, with other versions appearing into the 1600s with some differences. Once I started digging for gods with little info, Forseti popped up in a few places with woefully little definition. Jackpot—a god with a lot of blank whiteboards to build upon. The sacrifice was inspired by Christopher Moore's

"A Dirty Job" story, where there's a goth teen that keeps the protagonist on his toes. Wanting a similar foil and blending that with the Slenderman stabbing story from not long ago, I had my catalyst for controversy. The political angle came as I was outlining the story. We live at a time when everything gets politicized, which I am apparently guilty of now too. The similarities between the god characters and the politicians was too tempting for me to turn down, and the chance to lean into recent events was a fun challenge. If I pushed too far and it turned you off—you probably weren't my target audience. The contrast against Christianity and other Abrahamic religions such as Judaism and Islam became pretty obvious as I learned more about the Norse stories and I had my finale. Again, it's a work of fiction and I mean no harm.

How did you decide on translations / spellings / name usage?

A lot of research, seeing how various scholars translated, and personal taste. Where there's a name or word that is already popularized, I've stuck to those for readability, so Odin is not Othin, even if that is a closer translation. Hoth, however, I left as Hoth instead of Hoder, even though it's the same letter (ð or Eth) being translated. All cards on the table, this also means Idunn would have been pronounced closer to Ithun (kind of like Ethan).

I've left the -*r* off some names as well, as with Frey (Freyr), where I've left it on in the case of Balder (Baldr) for the same readability and popularity reasons. I can also hide that in the narrative that modern perceptions determine the reality of the gods so their names may have altered along with their appearances.

This was one of the encounters I had with the Tiffany Problem throughout the book. The Tiffany Problem states that even if something is historically accurate, its use may be disengaging for modern readers due to their perceptions of the past. Tiffany is a very old name, derived from Greek origins and popularized in the 12th century. But, if I were writing a historical fiction set in medieval Europe and called the princess Tiffany, the modern reader would hesitate. My first encounter was at the very first chapter, where Leif Erikson is known as the *steersman* and his second in command is called the s*kipper*. In modern terms, the skipper would be the one in charge, whereas on a Norse ship, the steersman was likely the person that owned the boat and was in charge. I hoped context would clear it up in that case.

If you're wondering why I went with Freyja instead of Freya—it's because I liked it better so deal with it. On that note, a common assumption is that

Frigg and Freyja are the same goddess. That may be, again our sources on Norse myth are fairly lean, but I prefer to think of them as separate, or at least separate aspects of the same deity. The Norse pantheon was assembled from a mishmash of beliefs as the Germanics spread north. Gods and goddesses were merged, changed aspects, changed names, and in some cases the pantheon got a bit bigger. Look at a list of Norse deities, there are so many fertility goddesses—which makes sense for an area that wasn't overly crop friendly. I allude to these disparate origins in the case of Hoth when Forseti is talking with Balder. In the Eddas, Balder is killed by Hoth, who is blind and tricked into piercing him with a mistletoe spear. In the Gesta Danorum, a Danish history that we get other stories such as Ragnar Lothbrok from, Balder stumbles across Nanna bathing and falls in love, though she is engaged to Hoth, a Danish hero. They fight a few times over her, even though Nanna said she didn't want Balder, and eventually Hoth kills Balder in battle.

A few Norse words I left untranslated and hoped it would either be picked up by context or close enough. In a couple of cases, I needed a good swear word, but didn't want to use English.

Argr—a derogatory statement meaning effeminate. I had Forseti use it when he was frustrated with himself for being weak, basically calling himself a bitch. Inappropriate, yes, but he's from a different time. It would have been odd to have him wake up and immediately use a modern expletive.

Hnefatafl—A board game popular among the Vikings that peaked in popularity in the Dark Ages. It's kind of like chess, if the one team started in the middle and the other team attacked from the edges. Kind of.

Flyting—A favorite pastime of the Norse gods, and one you may be familiar with if you played Assassin's Creed: Valhalla. Flyting was a poetry contest of insults. Imagine bearded Norse rap battling with each other, and you have it! Loki was a champion flyter and after one particularly notable exchange with Skadi, where he says he was first in line when the gods killed her father and then claimed she had begged him into her bed, Skadi promised that he would be bound to a rock with his own son's entrails. I can't find that she promised the snake part, but it served the story I was telling, and she is the one that hung the snake. If you want to see how great this flyting was, look up the poem Lokasenna (Loki's Taunts) which is part of the Poetic Edda.

Rassragr—One of the most offensive things you could call a Viking. In short it was someone who allowed themselves to be sodomized (the ragr prefix is the same root as argr above, so rass=arse and ragr=effeminate). Vikings didn't have any particular problem with gay sex from what I can tell, as long as you were the one giving. In typical dark ages self-loathing, the person receiving was the one worth humiliation. You can see why I used these insults without translation.

Völva—A woman who practices magic, a seeress or witch.

Skitr—Shit. Come on, that was an easy one.

Places

L'Anse aux Meadows is a real place on the northern tip of Newfoundland that is, in fact, the only known Viking settlement in North America outside Greenland. It likely served as a base for exploration for about 20 years before being abandoned. Its connection with Leif Erikson has been speculated as being from the Vinland sagas which served as jumping boards for the wine berry incident. The well part was my creation.

Dalhousie University is a real university in Halifax, Nova Scotia that is affiliated with University of King's College. I don't know if they have a professor of history that is also a medieval archaeologist or if they help to fund the Viking site.

Oubache State Park is a real place about an hour drive from Morgan and Megan's home in Indiana. It's not remarkable in any other way than I made sure to pick a real place.

Pop Culture Influences

It's undeniable that the superhero movies and recent games have changed the public's view of some of the more popular gods and their stories. While this made it fun to poke at the differences between old and new, it was unavoidable to draw comparisons and address parts of those films.

As I write this section, I am playing through God of War: Ragnarok, which just released, and there's a scene where you overhear people talking about Forseti. My blood froze. I couldn't have my unknown god main character having a presence in a AAA game! I stood and listened to the whole conversation. Luckily, it was filler background chatter that anyone that hadn't dedicated many hours to writing on would likely not even notice. Between the God of War games, Assassin's Creed game, and the superhero movies, the Norse pantheon is having an impressive reemergence. One I am glad to build on while trying to remain respectful to the source material.

About the Author

Michael Allen is a serial hobbyist that loves to pursue the things that appeal to him. Sci-Fi, RPGs, Fantasy, mythology, and historical fiction have long inspired him and have also helped connect him with many creative friends. In order to get his stories out, along with those of his friends and others, he began SthenoType. Combining many of his passions into his debut novel, *The Forgotten God*, he hopes to continue to write and pursue his passions. When he's not writing, he enjoys spending time with his family at their home in New Jersey.

CPSIA information can be obtained
at www.ICGtesting.com
Printed in the USA
BVHW050603270123
657224BV00010B/90

9 798987 377208